WHERE
DRAGONS
SOAR

WHERE DRAGONS SOAR

AND OTHER ANIMAL FOLK TALES
OF THE BRITISH ISLES

PETE CASTLE

No animals were harmed during the research for this book

Illustrations by Pete Castle

First published 2016

The History Press
The Mill, Brimscombe Port
Stroud, Gloucestershire, GL5 2QG
www.thehistorypress.co.uk

British Library Cataloguing in Publication Data.
A catalogue record for this book is available from the British Library.

ISBN 978 0 7509 6186 8

Typesetting and origination by The History Press
Printed in Great Britain

CONTENTS

ACKNOWLEDGEMENTS

As always thanks must go to my wife Sue for support, patience and practical assistance, and for just being there.

To Anni Plant for the back cover photo.

To Alan Wilkinson for permission to quote from his 'Hartlepool Monkey' song.

To The History Press and my editors for making the production of this book so easy.

To all the singers and storytellers who've influenced me over the years and to all the audiences who've supported me.

To the long line of storytellers who made and preserved these stories over countless millennia.

To my Facebook friends who suggested stories and subjects, some of which were used and some rejected.

INTRODUCTION

Stories are slippery creatures. You can't trust them.

They've been jumping on and off the page and into the mouths and ears of storytellers ever since time began. They've probably shared our hearths for far longer than dogs or cats or any other of our domestic animals. They don't stay put in one place either. If a group of people move you can guarantee that some stories will smuggle themselves away and move with them. Even if it's only a lone traveller visiting foreign parts, you can be sure a few stories will, like fleas, accompany him, and different ones will come back, so it's impossible to pin them down as belonging to any one particular place or people. As soon as you try – as soon as you say 'this story is native to this particular area' – then you are sure to find a very close relation to it living happily in another community, in another country, or even on another continent!

If you are a storyteller you might think stories are like cats – you don't choose them, they choose you! There were several stories I considered for inclusion here which refused to be pinned down. I offered them a home, but they just didn't want it. They slunk away.

This is a collection of *British* folk tales but how long they've been British, or whether they've always been British, is a matter for scholarship and debate. At the end of the last Ice Age Britain was empty, so we, and our stories, are all immigrants. We gradually moved here at different times from different places and brought our stories with us. It's impossible to draw a line and say the stories that came to Britain before that date are British and those that came after are imports, nor can we limit ourselves to stories that were invented on these shores because almost all stories are based on an idea from an older one.

So when deciding what to include, or not, it comes down to common sense. It's easy to make a case for including some 'imports' because they have become so well known that they are almost naturalised as British. The stories of the Grimms and other nineteenth-century continental collectors have entered our canon and are often better known to the general public than the work of, say, Joseph Jacobs in England. I've avoided those where there is an alternative, more local, version. There usually is!

I thought long and hard about whether or not to include any of the fables of Aesop. Everybody has heard of them and their morals; allusions to them or quotes from them have entered our everyday language (i.e. we all know of 'The Boy Who Cried Wolf'). They've been in print in English since they were published by Caxton in 1484 and have been retold over and over, but they are still known as 'Aesop's Fables' and are considered to be Greek, so I decided against them. But a couple managed to get in. I told you they were sneaky!

We need a perpetual supply of new stories to counteract the trickle of stories that get lost. Some are literally forgotten, sometimes they date and become difficult to understand, or they become untellable because of changing attitudes and social mores. Therefore I've allowed myself to introduce a handful here, in the hope that they fit and take root.

I once read that animal stories are amongst the oldest stories in the world. That is not surprising. Our early hominid ancestors, hunter-gatherers on the plains of Africa, were surrounded by other animals and once they had moved out of Africa and become meat eaters on the steppes and tundra they were dependent on animals for food and clothing, and sometimes fuel and building materials as well. I often picture the first story ever told was when a 'caveman' arrived back at his cave looking tattered and torn and told his family about the huge, ferocious beast he'd just escaped. In the way of 'fisherman's tales' the beast probably grew in repeated tellings and a mythological creature was born!

When the idea of this book was first suggested I leapt at it. I felt it was something I could really get my teeth into and enjoy doing (and I have!). Before I started any serious work on it I thought there would be so much material that I'd be spoiled for choice, that it might easily develop into two volumes ... or more. But once I'd started work I realised that wasn't quite the case. It's true that there are thousands of folk tales about animals and many of them are well known to everybody – both people who are fans of oral storytelling and the more general public. The question is, though, are there thousands which I could argue are *British* folk tales about animals and the answer to that is 'no'. Many of those that instantly spring to mind are European, or African, or American and definitely haven't been naturalised as British.

Bearing all that in mind, I hope you enjoy the selection I've made. I've striven for balance – balance of recent and ancient tales; balance of tales from different parts of the country (I've managed to include parts which often get forgotten, like the Isle of Man) and balance of all the different animals. An early idea I had was to restrict myself to 'animals', in the sense of mammals (with the odd dragon thrown in for flavour!) but I gradually realised that I should include fish and fowls as well – there is too much overlap not to. The only restriction I have kept to is that they should be stories *about* animals, not just stories in which animals play a small part. If there are no people involved so much the better!

I hope you approve of my selection. One of the first things I did was to ask my Facebook followers what animal legends they knew of; what towns had animals associated with them. Many of the replies mentioned three or four of the stories I have included here, but most were creatures associated with football teams which don't have any real 'story' to go with them. One of the most mentioned was 'The Derby Ram', but you won't find that here because I dealt with it at length in my *Derbyshire Folk Tales* book, where you can also find the story of 'The Bakewell Elephant'. I have included two stories from that book again here, though, because they were too important to miss – 'The Small-Tooth Dog' is probably the only British version of 'Beauty and the Beast', and 'The Derbyshire Werewolf' is one of very few British werewolf stories I've been able to find.

Several of the other stories have appeared, probably in slightly different form, in *Facts & Fiction* storytelling magazine, which I have edited since 1999. You might have heard me tell several of them as well.

Pete Castle,
Belper, Derbyshire,
2016

1

HERE BE DRAGONS

THE KNIGHT AND THE DRAGON

Once upon a time a knight met a dragon.
'I'm going to kill you,' said the knight.
'Oh, don't do that,' said the dragon, 'and I'll tell you a story.'
So he began:

Once upon a time a knight met a dragon.
'I'm going to kill you,' said the knight.
'Oh, don't do that,' said the dragon, 'and I'll tell you a story.'
So he began:

Once upon a time a knight met a dragon.
'I'm going to kill you,' said the knight.
'Oh, don't do that,' said the dragon, 'and I'll tell you a story.'
So he began:

Once upon a time a knight met a dragon.
'I'm going to kill you,' said the knight.
'Oh, don't do that,' said the dragon, 'and I'll tell you a story.'
So he began:

> Once upon a time a knight met a dragon … and so on for as long as you can bear it!

The most obviously ancient-seeming tales found in Britain are those about dragons and other mysterious beasts. (The fact that they are 'ancient-seeming' doesn't necessarily mean they are actually ancient, of course.) It seems logical to start this collection with a few of those.

Stories and legends about dragon-like creatures are found all over the British Isles, often just as fragments explaining, say, the circular ditches around a prehistoric hill fort (very likely called Worm Hill), but we tend to associate dragons mostly with Wales or Cornwall or the more remote parts of the north. 'Silly Sussex', then, is not the most obvious place to start this first section, but that's what we'll do. (Silly in this sense is from the Anglo-Saxon '*sælig*', meaning 'blessed'.)

A SUSSEX DRAGON

St Leonard's Forest is, today, part of the 'High Weald Area of Outstanding Natural Beauty'. It is a cosy, hospitable landscape which stretches from Surrey, through Sussex into Kent. It's typical 'Home Counties', 'Little England', England's 'green and pleasant land' personified. Above all, it is safe. But in the past it was the haunt of dragons!

Way back in the early years of the sixth century CE, St Leonard killed a dragon in the forest which was subsequently named after him. He was injured in the fray and lilies of the valley sprouted where his blood fell. (They still grow abundantly in some parts of the forest.)

He also banished all snakes from the area, but his cleansing was not absolutely perfect for, about a millennium later in 1614, a strange and dangerous creature was reported to be frequenting the overgrown hollows and 'vaultie places' of 'unwholesome shade' in the forest. Its home seems to have been near the village of Faygate but it was seen all over the area to within a few miles of the town of Horsham.

The creature was described as being a serpent or dragon about nine feet long, which left behind it a glutinous trail like that of a snail. The middle part of its body was thicker than the neck and tail, and there grew from its torso two large bunches 'about the size of footballs', which some people thought would eventually grow into wings. This suggests it was thought to be only a young dragon! The dragon was dark in colour, though the underneath tended to red, and round its neck it had a stripe of white scales. Descriptions are vague because the creature could only be seen from a distance.

Although it left behind it a snail-like trail it was by no means snail-like in its speed. If anyone dared to approach too close it would raise its neck and stare round, then, once it had spied its prey, it would race after them on its four stubby legs faster than a man could run. The dragon did not necessarily have to rely on its speed to catch his prey because from a distance of four rods (twenty metres) it could spit venom which caused the target to swell up and die. A man and woman who came upon the dragon by chance suffered in this way, as did the dogs set upon it by another man, as well as various cattle. Humans and cattle do not seem to have been the dragon's favoured food-stuffs, however. Although it killed them, it left them uneaten and seems to have preferred rabbits.

No one seems to know what happened to this creature and it disappeared from legend, although as late as the nineteenth century children were warned to keep out of various areas of the wood for fear of 'monstrous snakes'.

The source of this story is a pamphlet in the *Harleian Miscellany* with the wonderful title:

A True and Wonderful Discourse relating a strange and monstrous Serpent (or Dragon) lately discovered, and yet living, to the great Annoyance and divers Slaughters of both Men and Cattell, by his strong and violent Poison: in Sussex, two Miles from Horsam, in a Woode called St Leonard's Forrest, and thirtie Miles from London, this present Month of August, 1614. With the true Generation of Serpents.

With a title like that they didn't really need to write the story!

The Two Warring Dragons

After a cosy, almost domestic, start in Sussex, let's leap into classic 'dragon lore' for the next story. This is an ancient tale which has been told by many different people in many different times. Each telling is different and serves a different purpose – often political or nationalistic – depending upon the teller and the age. This is my telling, put together from various sources, which sets out to have no purpose other than to make a good story.

Way back in the earliest days of Britain, when there was no sense of one United Kingdom covering the whole island and no king who could command all the country; when there were no English and no Welsh; no Anglo-Saxons and no Celts; when the Romans had yet to bring their roads and walls and their Christian religion. Way back then, in the time of myths, there were two brother kings. Llefelys ruled a kingdom across the sea, in what we now call France, and his brother, Llud, ruled what is now southern England. They were good kings who ruled their kingdoms well and remained good friends. But Llud had a problem.

On the first day of every May, when his people should have been celebrating the end of winter with the raucous, bawdy, spring festival of Beltane, his kingdom was brought to a standstill by hideous screams and shrieks. These noises rang through the skies all over the kingdom and were impossible to ignore. They were so loud that they made the worst thunderstorm you have ever experienced seem tame and harmless. They were so terrible that they caused brave men to go pale and lose all their strength; lesser men lay down and died; women miscarried and animals became barren; the very crops in the fields withered and the new, fresh leaves fell from the trees.

Every year as Beltane approached, Llud's people grew scared and they shut themselves away where they hoped they wouldn't hear the screams – but there was nowhere to escape. They hoped and prayed to their gods that it wouldn't happen again this year, but it always did, and every year the kingdom fell further into rack and ruin. No one could explain the screams, or their effect, so no one knew what to do to counteract them.

One year, when things had reached a terrifying low, Llud went to his brother Llefelys for help, to see if he could offer any explanation. Llefelys had at his disposal all the best brains in Gaul and could summon help from all over the continent and soon he was able to explain Llud's problem. The shrieks and screams, he said, were caused by two dragons engaged in a never-ending battle. As they fought they roared out their pain and anger. To stop the disaster happening every year, Llud would have to stop the dragons fighting. They could not be killed, so he had to capture them and imprison them somewhere from which they could never escape.

Now that he knew what he must do Llud returned home and began making preparations to achieve his aim. The first task was to measure his kingdom from north to south and from east to west and find the dead centre. It turned out to be just outside the town of Oxford. There Llud had a huge watertight pit, or cistern, dug and when it was complete he filled it with mead. An enormous brocaded cloth was made to cover the pit.

On the eve of Beltane, Llud sat beside the pit and saw two terrifying, unimaginable beasts fighting. As they fought they changed. They went through every bloodthirsty animal known to man and many which aren't. They were bears, they were lions, they were basilisks and griffons. They became hounds and wolves, leopards and endless coiling snakes. They grew large, they shrunk small. They tried to trick each other. As the night grew old they changed into dragons and soared into the air to continue their fight. As they swooped and battled they let out the deadly shrieks which had ravaged his kingdom for so long.

After a night of fighting in which first one and then the other dragon had seemed to have the upper hand, they both sank to the ground by the cistern where they changed into giant pigs. Smelling the mead the pigs plunged into the pit and quenched their thirsts with gallons of the intoxicating liquid. Then they collapsed in a drunken stupor. Llud was then able to bind them up in the brocaded cloth and have them transported away to the distant mountains of North Wales, where they were interred in a cave far under the ground where they could do no more harm.

Llud became a hero to his people and ruled them well for the rest of his life. They thought that the threat of the warring dragons was a thing of the past and gradually the suffering they had caused faded from memory. Centuries passed and new peoples came to the country, new wars were fought and new kings ruled. One of these was called Vortigern. Vortigern had made his stronghold in the mountains of Caernarfon in North Wales on an isolated, rocky outcrop. He called it Dinas Ffaraon Dandde, or 'the fortress of the fiery pharaoh'. From there he ruled a wide area of land, but in order to make himself stronger and even more powerful he needed to expand and strengthen his castle. The trouble was, every time he constructed a new tower or a new wall, it cracked and tumbled down.

Vortigern consulted his advisors, all the wisest sages and cleverest magicians he had at his disposal, and they told him that the only remedy was to find a boy who had no natural father and to sacrifice him. But what kind of boy has no natural father? Vortigern eventually found one, a young lad called Merlin whose father was a demon or shapeshifter, so he was

'no natural father'. Although he wasn't a shapeshifter like his father, Merlin did have more than natural powers and he was able to explain that Vortigern's advisors were wrong. Sacrificing him would make no difference. The towers and walls kept falling down, he said, because the castle was built over a vast cave in which two warring dragons were trapped. It was their writhing which shook the ground and caused the towers to fall.

Following Merlin's advice Vortigern ordered his men to dig, and sure enough they opened up a huge underground cavern from which two vast dragons, one red, one white, soared into the skies and continued their age-long battle. All the people were terrified and fled, except Merlin, who stood by the cavern applauding them on. Eventually one of the dragons was defeated and fell to earth, where it died. The other gave a great roar of victory, transformed itself into a huge serpent and crawled off into the earth to await a time when it might return to aid one or other of the peoples of these islands.

Whether the victor was the red dragon of Wales or the white dragon of England depends, of course, on who is telling the story, so I'll leave that to you to decide for yourself.

When is a Dragon a Worm?

The previous story depicts the classic dragon: a gigantic creature with wings, which flies through the air, breathing fire down on to its enemies and collects to itself a hoard of gold that it then guards jealously. That kind of dragon is sometimes found in British folklore, particularly in Welsh tales. It is also the kind of dragon that occurs in more recent fantasy fiction, from Tolkien onwards.

But the real British dragon is a worm – sometimes spelled 'wurm' or 'wyrm'. The word comes from the Germanic languages and is the word for a serpent, a snake or a dragon. (I once stayed for a very short night at a hotel near the German/Austrian border called Hotel Wurm, which had as its sign a sort of 'St George and the Dragon' type picture. As I said, it was a very short night, they didn't speak English and I don't speak German, so I didn't find out whether there was a local legend attached to it, but I'd bet there was. It's a story found worldwide.)

There are plenty of worms in British folklore and it is quite a commonplace name. A quick look at major places in the road atlas comes up with about twenty towns and villages starting with Worm ... some of those are thought to be named after a man named Worm/Wyrm (in other words they are Mr Worm's town), rather than after creatures, but about half are places where snakes were found – Wormwood Scrubs being a prime example.

There is a Worm Hill near Washington in Tyne and Wear, and that is associated with this next famous tale ...

THE LAMBTON WORM

Young Sir John Lambton was the heir to his family fortune and a large estate in County Durham. But he was not interested in estates, and only in fortunes if they meant that he could enjoy himself. Rather than study he preferred to hunt, and rather than go to church on Sunday he preferred to go fishing in the nearby River Wear. That is what he did one fateful Sunday.

On his way to the river young Sir John met one of his father's old retainers, a man who had known him since he was a toddler so wasn't scared of giving him a word of advice. He warned John that no good would come of fishing on a Sunday and he should go back and go to church as all respectable people do. John ignored the old man and went down to the river and set up his gear. It was a perfect morning for fishing and John was a skilled fisherman, but that morning he could catch nothing. (If you are a fisherman I expect you have had mornings like that.)

He could catch nothing ... that is, until he heard the distant church bell ring out the end of the service and at that very moment he felt a tug on the line. Only a small tug, it's true, and when he pulled it in he found on his hook a strange little creature, more like a worm than a fish. It was not much bigger than his thumb and it had nine tiny holes down each side of its head. John didn't know what it was, he'd never seen a fish like it, but he was fascinated by it, so he took it home with him in a jug. By the time he'd got home, though, he'd lost interest. The fish wasn't all that fascinating so he tipped it into a well.

Soon Sir John Lambton went off with other young men of similar rank to fight in the wars in Palestine – the Crusades. They were all hoping for excitement and glory. They wanted riches and adventures and Crusading seemed the surest way of finding them. They were gone for many years.

In the years that Sir John Lambton was away that little worm in the well grew and grew until it was too big for the well and it crawled off to live in the River Wear. At night it would come out and eat all the livestock it could find – cows and sheep and, if it was really hungry, it would rear up its head, poke it through the window of a house, and take small children sleeping in their cradles. Sometimes it would spend the day lazing in the sun with its tail curled round Penshaw Hill, or the nearby hill which now bears its name – Worm Hill.

Word of the monster worm spread near and far and many warriors came and attempted to win themselves glory by killing it. They all failed because any part of the worm they chopped off immediately joined back on and it became whole again. Even if a knight managed to chop the worm in half the two halves always managed to rejoin.

After many years in the Holy Land, Sir John Lambton returned home to find his estates in ruins and his lands barren and empty because of the depredations of the worm. He went into Durham and consulted an old wise woman who advised him on how he should set about killing the worm.

Following her advice, Sir John covered his armour with sharp spikes so that when the worm tried to coil round him parts of it would be cut off. He then went to face it in the middle of the River Wear so that the parts which came off would be swept away by the current and could not rejoin. The old woman also told Sir John that after he had killed the worm he should be sure to kill the first living thing he saw. If he failed to do this, a curse would fall upon his family and none of them would die peacefully in their beds for nine generations. To prevent this from happening Sir John arranged with his father that when the worm was dead he would sound his horn three times. His father would then loose young John's hunting hound, which would run to him and be sacrificed.

Young Sir John Lambton put on his spiky armour, took the huge two-handed sword he'd used to good effect in the Holy Land and taunted the worm into fighting him in the middle of the fast-flowing river. Every time it coiled round him parts were cut off and washed away and Sir John hacked off other parts. Gradually the worm grew smaller and smaller and weaker and weaker, and then the battle was over and the worm was no more. Young Sir John took his horn and blew the three blasts of victory. His father heard them, but in his excitement he forgot all about the hound and ran to embrace his son himself. Young Sir John could not bear to kill his own father and so the curse fell upon the family. Old and young Sir John Lambton both died in tragic circumstances, as did their descendants for nine generations. The last of those, Sir Henry Lambton, died in his carriage while crossing Lambton Bridge in 1761.

Whisht! lads, haad yor gobs,
An' aa'll tell ye aall an aaful story,
Whisht! lads, haad yor gobs,
An' aa'll tel ye 'boot the worm.

Back in the 1970s, when I first got into folk music, the song of the Lambton Worm was often sung in the clubs, usually with an excruciatingly bad Geordie accent. It is an old legend that Joseph Jacobs used, which inspired a pantomime and influenced several novels, including Bram Stoker's The Lair of the White Worm, *which is so bad it's good!*

ASSIPATTLE AND THE
MUCKLE MESTER STOORWORM

A Story from the Far North

Assipattle was the seventh son of a seventh son, but there seemed very little else that was special about him. All day long his father and brothers herded cattle and in the evening they sat in the kitchen and whittled spoons from cow horn. All day long, while they worked, Assipattle lay on the ash pile by the fire with his hands behind his head, dreaming of the day when he would marry a princess and inherit a castle and have lands to rule. His parents shook their heads over him and his brothers kicked him and cursed him for a fool and a lazy good-for-nothing.

The farm belonging to Assipattle's father lay in the very north of the country, close to the roaring river that girds the world. In that river, swimming like a monstrous eel against the current, lived the muckle mester Stoorworm. The Stoorworm was one of the nine fearful curses that plague mankind. Its eyes were like lakes, its teeth were like precipices, and its tail was long enough to wrap right around the earth. Its breath was so venomous that when it was angry and blew out a loud gust, every living thing for miles around fell down dead. When it felt hungry the Stoorworm heaved its head on to the land, flicked out its forked tongue and began swallowing human beings like a lizard swallows flies.

The Stoorworm's favourite food was children, and every year the soldiers of Assipattle's country tied up seven boys and seven girls like parcels and left them on the beach for the Stoorworm to eat. This went on for many years and gradually there came to be fewer and fewer children in the land. Eventually, the only child left in the whole country was the king's own daughter, Gem-de-Lovely, a princess just turned fourteen.

'Send messengers all around the kingdom,' commanded the
king, 'and if a champion can be found to kill the Stoorworm,
his reward will be my daughter's hand in marriage, and a castle
and lands to rule.'

'What if we find no champion, highness?' asked the messengers.

'Then I'll fight the beast myself,' said the king.

The messengers rode out and champions from every corner
of the kingdom came and gathered at the king's castle. At first
there were 333 of them, feasting and drinking all at the king's
expense. But as time passed and the day of the contest came
nearer, some of them quietly sneaked away. A week before
the fight only thirty-three were left; three days after that there
were just three; and two days later there were none. The king
ordered his royal boat to be moored by the shore ready to ferry
him to fight the Stoorworm, and his royal armour to be fetched
out and polished. It would either protect him or it would make
a grand funeral costume.

On the evening before the fight Assipattle was dozing on the
ash pile as usual when he heard his mother and father talking.
'Get out my best clothes,' his father said, 'and make sure that
the horse Teetgong is saddled and bridled, for as soon as it is
dawn I am going to watch the king fight the Stoorworm.'

'How can I bridle Teetgong?' asked the wife. 'He won't stand
still for anyone but you.'

'If you want him to stand still you pat his right shoulder;
if you want him to prance you stroke his left ear; and if you
want him to gallop you blow on that goose-quill whistle in my
pocket,' said her husband.

Assipattle lay still and when everyone else was asleep he filled
a porridge pot with embers from the fire, took the goose-quill
whistle from his father's pocket and crept to the stable. At first
Teetgong shied and reared but he patted the horse on his right

shoulder and at once he stood quiet while Assipattle saddled and bridled him. Assipattle climbed into the saddle and stroked Teetgong's left ear and the horse pranced out into the moonlight. The clatter of hooves woke Assipattle's father and brothers and they ran out to catch the thief, but before they could even mount their horses Assipattle blew the goose-quill whistle and Teetgong galloped away as fast as the wind.

When they came to the coast Assipattle patted Teetgong's neck, jumped down and let him loose to graze on the headland. Not far out to sea was what looked like a dark, green island, breathing gently. It was the Stoorworm's head. Bobbing in the bay beside the shore was the king's royal boat. Assipattle put the pot of embers down and began gathering driftwood and dry seaweed. The boatman heard the rustle of wood and weed, woke up and said, 'What are you doing?'

'Lighting a fire,' said Assipattle. 'Why not step ashore and warm yourself?'

'I can't do that,' said the boatman, 'suppose someone sneaked up while I was ashore and stole this boat?'

'Please yourself,' said Assipattle. He cleared the fireplace and then began scrabbling at the earth and shouting, 'Stay away! Stay away!'

'What's the matter now?'

'Nothing! Stay away! I never mentioned gold!' said Assipattle.

As soon as the ferryman heard the word 'gold' he splashed ashore and began scrabbling in the dirt of Assipattle's fireplace. Assipattle snatched up the pot of embers, jumped into the boat and set sail for the Stoorworm, leaving the boatman waving his fists in the air and cursing.

The sun was just rising and its rays shone full into the Stoorworm's face and wakened it. The Stoorworm opened its jaws and yawned, and the yawn sucked a great cataract of seawater into its mouth and down its throat. Assipattle set his course straight for the gap, and the current drew him in under the Stoorworm's teeth, into its cavern-mouth and on down its throat with a mass of seaweed, dead fish and ship's planking rushing along beside him. At last the boat grounded on a shelf of flesh and Assipattle threw out his anchor, hauled down his sail and splashed out to explore the Stoorworm's innards.

Using the pot of coals to light his path he threaded his way along the Stoorworm's inside passages and tunnels like a man in a labyrinth, and at last he came to the liver, hanging overhead like an enormous purple cliff. Assipattle clambered up it till he found a fold, emptied the potful of embers into it and blew on them to make them glow. The liver-oils spluttered, burst into flame, and soon the Stoorworm's whole liver was sizzling like roasting meat. As quickly as he could Assipattle ran back to his boat and hauled up the anchor. Just in time.

The Stoorworm felt the fire burning deep inside. The pain made it writhe and gulp down water to quench the heat. Assipattle's boat spun like a twig in a torrent, and he clung to the mast while the torrent roared all round him. At last, with a massive heave, the Stoorworm opened its mouth and spewed out a mouthful of water that carried Assipattle, his boat, and all the children the Stoorworm had ever swallowed on to the beach for, by some miracle, they hadn't died but had been able to live deep down in the Stoorworm's innards.

The Stoorworm continued to lash and writhe, snorting steam and fire. Then the flames reached the very centre of its liver and at last, overcome by agony, it flung itself out of the sea and reached up with its tongue to snatch the moon from the sky to crush the fire. But the tongue missed its target and just snapped off one of the moon's horns and sent it crashing to earth. The Stoorworm fell with it and broke into pieces as it fell.

The Stoorworm's tongue made a trench between the countries of Denmark and Sweden, and seawater rushed in to fill it. Where the tongue landed became the Baltic Sea. The teeth fell from its jaws and made the islands we call the Orkneys and Shetland, and its tail-splinters made the Faroes. With its dying strength, the monster coiled its body into a ball and sank like a stone to the bed of the northern sea. Even then, it was so huge that its back stuck up above the surface of the ocean in the shape of the country we now call Iceland, and to this very day, its liver-fires continue to blaze under the ground and sometimes erupt out in spectacular displays of molten rock and smoke.

As soon as the Stoorworm's death-agony ended and the smoke cleared, Assipattle mounted Teetgong, stroked the horse's left ear and led a procession of rescued children to the king's palace. There, he asked for princess Gem-de-Lovely's hand in marriage. The king dressed Assipattle in a crimson robe and girded the sword Sikkersnapper, which had been handed down from Odin himself, round his waist. Then Assipattle and Gem-de-Lovely were married and such a wedding had never been seen.

Assipattle's dreams had come true, he had a wife, a castle and lands to rule; lands which stretched north, south, east and west. Assipattle's father and brothers also prospered, for they set up a quarry in the place where the moon's horn had fallen to earth and their cow-horn spoons gave way to moon-horn spoons which were famous in those parts ever afterwards.

Assipattle and Gem-de-Lovely lived happily ever after and had many fine children and, if they are not dead, they are living yet …

This story from Orkney is not far removed from the Norse creation myth, in which the world was created from the body of Ymir when he was slain by Odin, Vili and Vé. There were many Stoorworms, or sea serpents, but this one was the 'mester' or master, i.e. the largest. Assipattle is a nickname for someone who likes to laze in the warmth of the fire rather than go about their business. You will find many such people in folk tales.

Nessie, the Loch Ness Monster

Now we are established on our way through this exploration of the animal kingdom, but before we leave dragons and move on to more homely creatures, let's consider what is arguably the best-known serpent of all. Nessie, the Loch Ness monster, is surely one of the most famous monsters in the world – and one of the best loved. She, for it is usually considered to be a

she, has earned a friendly nickname and her image, in a cuddly, smiley form, is used to sell everything from tourism to trinkets. She is an ad-man's dream! But this was not always the case.

Stories of water monsters (often called 'kelpies') have been common for as long as anyone knows – in rivers, lakes and lochs, as well as in the seas all round Britain; but particularly so in Scotland. The first mention of a monster in the Loch Ness area dates back to the sixth century CE, but on that occasion it was in the river which flows into the loch rather than in Loch Ness itself.

The story goes that the Irish monk and missionary St Columba was travelling through the land of the Picts when he came across a group of people burying a man beside the River Ness. When Columba asked what had happened they explained that he had been swimming in the river when a water beast had attacked him and dragged him under. They had tried to rescue him with a boat but had failed and were only able to retrieve his dead body. To their amazement St Columba then ordered his friend and companion, Luigne moccu Min, to jump in and swim across the river. Moccu Min may have been surprised, and was probably frightened, but he did as he was asked and dived in. He had not gone far when the beast appeared and made for the man. Everyone was horrified and expected moccu Min to meet the same fate as the man whose body they had just found, but St Columba made the sign of the cross and commanded, 'Go no further. Leave the man alone. Return from whence you came!'

The beast stopped as if restrained by ropes, then turned and swam off at top speed. Both St Columba's followers and the pagan Picts gave thanks and praised God.

No more was heard of a Loch Ness monster for over 1,000 years, until 14 April 1933 in fact, when John Mackay and his wife spotted 'something resembling a whale' as they drove past the loch. Was it coincidence that this happened in 1933, or was there 'something in the air', for it was also in 1933 that the original version of the film *King Kong* was released! Monsters were the fashion. Perhaps it was a relief from the miseries of the economic situation?

Ever since then 'monster mania' has gripped the region and the whole of the local economy is based on it through tourism and monster hunting. The image of the creature has gradually coalesced to become a form of plesiosaur, although that does not really make sense of the sightings on the loch shore …

The story of St Columba is found in Adomnán of Iona's *Life of Columba* which was copied at Iona during, or shortly after, Adomnán's lifetime.

Many other saints had dealings with 'wurms' or snakes, most notably St Patrick. Naturalists will tell you that there have never been snakes in Ireland as there was no way for them to colonise the island after the Ice Age, but legend tells that they were there until St Patrick banished them.

A very similar tale is told of St Hilda of Whitby. She used a whip to cut off their heads and their remains can still be found on the beach. (They are, of course, fossil ammonites.)

2

MAN'S BEST FRIEND

Dogs are generally considered to be 'man's best friend'. They were, arguably, the first animals to be domesticated and have continued to be one of the favourite pets and most useful assistants in all kinds of fields, from guarding to hunting and tracking; for transport; for use as hand warmers; as eyes, ears and even, in some places, as food!

People have always wondered how and when the first dogs were domesticated. In the past it was thought that various species of dogs were tamed at different times in different places in prehistory, but now, since the dog's genome has been mapped, it has been proved that all dogs, whether they are St Bernards or Chihuahuas, are descended from wolves.

One of the dog's most valued assets is faithfulness and that is illustrated in these next two stories, which both claim to be true … but almost certainly aren't! (In fact, both could be described as scams designed to boost tourism!)

GREYFRIARS BOBBY

If you've ever been on the tourist trail in Edinburgh you've probably visited the famous statue of Greyfriars Bobby which stands at the corner of Candlemaker's Row and the George IV Bridge, in the centre of the city. It is one of the 'must see' sights.

Bobby was a Skye terrier owned by John Gray, a night-watchman in the city. When John Gray died he was buried in Greyfriars Kirkyard and Bobby took up residence on his grave. He stayed there for the next fourteen years until he, too, died in 1872. His faithfulness so impressed people that Lady Burdett-Coutts had the statue erected so that he would be remembered. (Some people have dared to suggest that there were several Bobbies over the years and when one died or disappeared he was surreptitiously replaced because he attracted sightseers! But no one would dare do that, would they?)

GELERT, THE FAITHFUL HOUND

The village of Beddgelert (pronounced Beth-GEL-ert, with the accent on the GEL) is in Snowdonia in North Wales about halfway between Porthmadog and Snowdon itself. It is in the heart of the Snowdonia tourist area and is visited by thousands of people every year, many of whom come because of this famous story. It was a story much beloved by the Victorians and it can be found in many old books for children.

Prince Llewelyn the Great, also known as Llywelyn ap Lorwerth or Llywelyn Fawr, married Princess Joan, a daughter of King John of England, and part of the dowry was a fine wolfhound named Gelert. Llewelyn and Gelert became insepa-rable – I suspect that he might have loved the dog more than he loved Joan! Gelert was a fine hunting dog, fierce and fearless. He would face up to a wolf or boar, or drag down a deer and enjoy it as much as his master. He was also very protective of his master and of his master's property.

One day Llewelyn went hunting in the nearby forest. They had a good day, but at some stage Llewelyn realised that Gelert had gone missing. Llewelyn wasn't too worried; he assumed the dog had gone off on an errand of his own, chasing a boar or sniffing out an interesting trail. He was sure he would make his own way home some time.

Late that afternoon Llewelyn arrived back at his castle and strode into the hall to find it in chaos: the rushes on the floor were scattered all around and piled in heaps, their dust filled the room and hung in the air; tapestries had been torn from the walls and pictures hung askew; tables and benches were over-turned and cushions and drapes lay in random piles. There was no sign of his wife, but in one corner of the room was the cradle in which he expected to find his son. It was upside down and beside it lay bloodstained covers. For a split second Llewelyn imagined that the castle must have been attacked by outlaws, but then Gelert came whimpering and cowering from behind a piece of furniture.

The dog's face and jaws were covered in blood and a piece of cloth Llewelyn recognised as belonging in the baby's cot was draped across his back. Gelert cowered and behaved as dogs do when they know they have done something likely to offend their master. Llewelyn didn't have to think, he knew what had happened, his faithful Gelert had been overcome by jealousy, had run home and had attacked and killed the baby. In a split second Llewelyn drew his sword and plunged it into the dog's side.

Gelert's dying whimper was echoed by another similar sound from under the upturned cradle. Llewelyn dragged it aside and there, unharmed, was his baby son. And sticking out from under the drapery was the leg of another animal. Llewelyn pulled the covers aside and found the body of a huge wolf covered in blood and wounds. He could only imagine the tremendous fight which had taken place as Gelert saved his son from the ferocious beast.

Llewelyn collapsed in tears of grief and joy mixed in fairly equal proportions. His son was alive, but it was too late to do anything to save Gelert who was already dead. Llewelyn is said never to have smiled again, but he built the grave to his faithful dog so that its bravery would be remembered for ever – the grave that is now visited by so many tourists. The story has caught the imagination of many generations of people from that day on.

The main events of this story are found in the folk tales of many countries in Europe and even further afield – in India, a similar tale features a mongoose and a snake. It is possibly one of man's oldest tales.

The village of Beddgelert was probably named after the early Christian saint, Celert or Kilart, rather than the mythical dog, but in the late seventeenth century David Pritchard, the landlord of the Goat Hotel, heard the story of the faithful hound and used it to entice travellers to the village. He was the person responsible for building the grave on which you can find the bare bones of the story.

Black Shuck and Other Spectral Dogs

Black Shuck is the name given, loosely, to various spectral black dogs. It is often referred to as an East Anglian phenomenon, and that is where the name comes from, but stories of similar ghostly dogs are found all over the country. I included one in my book, *Nottinghamshire Folk Tales*. Here are some more. But first let's set the scene and build an atmosphere …

If you are walking home late in the evening, in the pitch dark of a country lane, with the wind rustling in the hedgerows and the unidentifiable sounds of nature all around you, you may be forgiven for feeling apprehensive, or even downright scared! If you then become aware that some of those sounds seem to be the padding footsteps of a large animal which is following you, you'd be very unimaginative if you weren't scared. In fact, you could be forgiven for screaming and running as fast as you could ... except that would probably do you no good at all because you couldn't outrun it, could you? Whatever it was.

If you are in East Anglia, the creature which is following you might well be Black Shuck. Black Shuck is a huge black dog, sometimes with just one eye, 'as big as a dinner plate', as Hans Anderson would have it, in the middle of its forehead.

Shuck might be out to harm you, but more likely he will ignore you as if your world and his do not meet. Sometimes, though, he has been known to help – to guide you home, particularly if you are a woman or are lost.

The Suffolk Black Dogs

One of the earliest accounts we have of Black Shuck is from Suffolk and this time he was definitely not in a helpful mood!

It was 4 August 1577, a Sunday, and the villagers of Blythburgh in Suffolk were all at their morning worship. Suddenly there was a huge crack of thunder and the doors of the church flew open. A huge black dog burst in and ran up the nave of the church, killing a man and a boy and causing the church steeple to collapse through the roof! Then it turned and ran out of the church again, leaving scorch marks on the door, which can still be seen!

Later that same day, at nearby Bungay, something similar happened. There was a large congregation all at prayer when the dog burst in and ran down the church in a storm of fire. He killed several people as he passed and when he reached the choir he turned and slew many more before disappearing back the way he'd come.

THE AYLESBURY BLACK DOG

There was a man who lived in a village near Aylesbury in Buckinghamshire who made his living as a dairyman. He kept several cows which he'd milk morning and night, and he'd then sell the milk around the locality. To get to the field where he kept his cows he regularly took a shortcut across a neighbour's field. One night, as he was approaching the gap in the hedge through which he always went, he saw a big black dog sitting there. He wasn't at all scared of dogs, but this one was very large and very fierce-looking, and it glared at him with fiery, threatening eyes. It was so threatening that the dairyman was not sure whether it was a dog or a fiend, so he turned aside and went through the gate at the end of the field instead. From then on the dog was there every night, barring his way, and every night the dairyman turned aside and went through the gate instead of through the gap in the hedge which would have been much quicker.

Then, one night, on his way back home after milking, he fell in with an old mate and they walked along together. As they did so the dairyman told his friend about the dog and, feeling brave because he was not alone this time, he vowed that he would see it off. As they crossed the field they saw the dog looking larger and more threatening than ever. His eyes gleamed in the moonlight and they could see spittle dripping from his lips.

The dairyman did not want to back down in front of his friend so he put down the pails of milk which he was carrying on a yoke, and walked towards the dog waving the yoke and shouting, 'Be off, you black fiend, or we'll see what you are made of!' The dog did not move and so the dairyman, trembling with fear, stepped towards it and swung the yoke …

at nothing. There was no dog there. The dog had vanished and the dairyman fell down in a swoon. He was carried home alive but never regained his senses. The dog was never seen again.

THE BLACK DOG OF LYME REGIS

There once was a large mansion stood in its own grounds on the edge of Lyme Regis in Dorset. It was a rich, important building and because of that it was attacked and destroyed during the English Civil War. The strongest part of a house is often the wall containing the main chimney, and that was the situation here. After the war only the end of the house with the chimney and the hearth and just a few other bits of wall stood up out of the rubble. This was repaired and reroofed and it was used as a farmhouse.

Several generations of farmers lived there with no trouble, but then a ghostly black dog began to appear, sitting by the hearth. It did no harm, it just sat there and the family became used to it. It was almost like a very easy-to-care-for family pet! But other local people were worried about this haunting and they taunted the farmer and bullied him until he agreed to do something to lay the ghost. The next night he came home drunk and, seeing the dog sitting there as usual, he grabbed the poker and lunged at the dog with it. The dog ran off and he chased it up the stairs and into the attic where it disappeared through the wall. As it disappeared the farmer swiped at it with the poker, missed, and made a hole in the ceiling. A cloud of dust and rubbish fell down and amidst it all was an old box. When the farmer opened it he found it was full of ancient gold coins dating back to pre-Civil War days.

From that day on the dog was never again seen in the house, but it was regularly seen in the lane outside the farm at midnight. The lane became known as 'Dog Lane'. Today, on the maps it is called Hayes Lane, but locals still call it Dog Lane and newcomers and holidaymakers are warned not to let their dogs stray at night for, if they do, they tend to disappear.

The farmer used the gold coins to buy a nearby property, which he opened as a pub – the Black Dog Inn near Uplyme. The Black Dog did good trade for many years but was demolished in 1916 because the building had become unsafe. A new property was built on the site and is currently trading as The Old Black Dog B&B, so although the dog itself disappeared, its memory lingers on.

The Black Dog of the Wild Forest

Once upon a time there was a king and a queen and they had one son who they called Jack, which wasn't a very good name for a prince, it's the kind of name usually given to a farm boy or a simpleton, but Jack he was, so Jack he will remain. When Jack was born it was foretold that when he came of age he would be eaten by the Black Dog of the Wild Forest. This did not worry anyone very much at the time because it seemed a long way in the future and you never know what is going to happen, but as his coming of age drew nearer and nearer, the king (and the queen as well, I expect) became sad and apprehensive, as they were very fond of their son.

At last, when the fateful day was nearly upon them, Jack's father, the king, gave the boy the best horse from out of his stable and as much money as he could carry, and sent him on his way. He doubted whether the boy could escape his fate, but he told him to try.

Jack rode as fast as he could for hundreds and hundreds of miles until night started to fall. Then he saw a small light glimmering in the distance, perhaps 100 miles off, so he rode on until he came to a house. It was a witch's house.

The witch welcomed him and said 'Come in king's son. I know your fate and why you are here. I doubt I can help you, but I will try.' She put him in the ash hole – the rubbish hole under the fire – to hide, and then she went away.

Jack had only been in the ash hole for about twenty minutes when there was a commotion outside, the door of the house flew open, and in rushed the Black Dog of the Wild Forest howling and breathing fire out of his mouth. He was followed by the old witch and her little dog, who set upon the Black Dog of the Wild Forest. The witch beat him and the dog bit him until he ran away.

'You can come out now,' she said. 'This is my little dog Hear-All and we have chased your enemy away. It's safe for you to come out and have something to eat.' The witch gave Jack a delicious meal and, in return, he gave her a lot of money. Then she said that she had a sister who lived about 300 miles away. If the boy could get there then she might be able to tell him how he could avoid his fate. 'To help you on your way,' she said, 'I will give you the bread out of my mouth and my little dog Hear-All.'

So Jack got on his horse and galloped away with the little dog Hear-All running beside him, and he rode and he rode until he felt his horse growing tired. He slowed and looked back and there was a speck in the distance. It was the Black Dog of the Wild Forest getting closer and closer. He galloped on until he came to the second sister's house.

Once again Jack was hidden in the ash hole while the witch went to do battle with the Black Dog of the Wild Forest, and if they had fought hard the first night they fought many times harder the second. When the Black Dog of the Wild Forest had been sent scuttling off the witch fed Jack and said, 'My young prince, I will do for you as well as I can: I will give you my dog Spring-All and I will give you this rod. Now mark well what I tell you – you must follow this ball of wool and it will lead you straight to a river. When you reach the river you must strike the water with the rod and, straight away, a bridge will spring up. Cross the bridge and immediately strike the water again and the bridge will disappear. Don't forget, and the Black Dog of the Wild Forest will not be able to follow you across.'

So Jack rolled the ball of wool and followed after it in the direction it showed him. Soon he heard panting behind him and he could see the Black Dog of the Wild Forest racing after him, but he reached the river and struck the water with the rod. Immediately a bridge like a rainbow sprung up across the river and Jack galloped over. When he reached the other side he remembered to strike the water again and the bridge faded into nothingness just as the Black Dog of the Wild Forest was about to step on to it.

Jack now found himself in a thick forest and the further he rode into it the thicker and thicker and wilder and wilder it became. He feared he would be lost forever and die in this wilderness, but at last he came out into a clearing, and there stood a castle. Jack went and knocked on the door of the castle and was invited in and made welcome. The next day the king of the castle took Jack hunting and they killed many birds and several creatures – it was a good day's hunting.

Now the king had a daughter, and Jack and the daughter liked each other immediately. She told Jack that the thing the king most desired was a bridge over the river which would make life in his castle very much easier. So he took her down to the bank to show her what he could do with his rod. She was very impressed, and was so intent on showing Jack how pleased she was with the bridge that he forgot to make it disappear again, and that night the Black Dog of the Wild Forest came over the bridge and went to the castle and made itself known to the queen.

Now the queen did not like Jack and she definitely did not want Jack to win the heart of her daughter, so she listened to what the Black Dog of the Wild Forest had to say. He told her that Jack would be going hunting in the forest again the next morning and that he planned to attack and kill him there. But he needed the queen's help. He told her to fasten Jack's two little dogs, Hear-All and Spring-All, in the cellar so that they couldn't follow.

'I will follow Jack into the forest,' said the Black Dog of the Wild Forest, 'and I will attack him there, and Jack will kill me and bring me back draped over the saddle of his horse. When you see this you must ask what he is going to do with my body and Jack will say he is going to burn it. And Jack will burn my body to dust. Then you must get a small stick and poke around in the ashes until you find a small bone – a lucky bone – and you must take it and, when Jack is asleep, you must drop it into his ear. Then Jack will be dead and you can take him and bury him and you'll never see or hear any more of him.'

The next morning Jack and the king went hunting again and Jack called and called to his little dogs Hear-All and Spring-All, but they didn't come and Jack was worried for them. And then along came the Black Dog of the Wild Forest who attacked Jack and, after a terrible fight, Jack slew the Black Dog of the Wild Forest and draped it across the front of his saddle and set off back to the castle.

When he reached the castle the queen came out to meet him and saw the body of the Black Dog of the Wild Forest hanging from Jack's saddle and she asked him what he was going to do with it. 'I'm going to burn it,' said Jack. 'Burn it to dust.' And he did, and then he retired to bed and the queen took a stick and scratched through the ashes of the fire until she found a small bone – a lucky bone – and she took it and crept into Jack's room where he lay sleeping and she dropped the lucky bone into his ear, and in the morning Jack appeared to be dead, so they took him and placed him in a coffin and they buried him in the graveyard.

A few days later, the parson saw two little dogs moping around by the side of Jack's grave and asked whose they were. When he learned that they were Jack's he decided that they needed to raise the coffin up and look inside it – and there was Jack lying dead. But little Hear-All leapt into the coffin and licked the bone out of Jack's ear and Jack sprang up as well as could be.

Jack went back to the castle, where he killed the queen and married the princess. Then, with his bride beside him, he mounted his horse and galloped off towards to his own land and his parents. As he was riding along, little dog Hear-All, who was running alongside his horse, said to Jack, 'Come down and cut off my head.'

'I couldn't do that,' said Jack, 'for all the kindnesses you've done for me.'

'If you don't then I will eat both you and your bride,' said little dog Hear-All, so Jack jumped down and cut off little dog Hear-All's head. He rode on a bit further, crying for the loss of little dog Hear-All when little dog Spring-All called out, 'Jack, stop and come down and do the same to me or I will eat both you and your bride.' So Jack stopped and cut off little dog Spring-All's head.

Jack and the princess had not ridden much further, all the time lamenting the loss of the two little dogs, when they heard riders behind them and they were met by the two most handsome ladies they had ever seen. 'Why are you crying?' asked the ladies, and Jack told them it was for the loss of his two faithful little dogs.

'Would you know them if you met them again?' asked the ladies, and Jack assured them that he would. But he was mistaken, because one of the ladies said, 'I am little Hear-All and this is little Spring-All and we will be happy to go with you.' And they all rode back to Jack's parents' castle where he and his wife lived happily and little Hear-All and little Spring-All lived with them as their faithful friends and companions.

3

AS WILD AS A WOLF, AS WILY AS A FOX

Wolves

In folk tales members of the dog family are often interchangeable. In different places the same story appears, but with a different animal named – here it is a fox, there it is a jackal; here a wolf, there a coyote …

Man's relationship with the wolf has always been 'difficult' – fear alternates with awe. It's hard to say when wolves became

extinct in Britain, for they died out at different times in different parts of the country. Wolves probably died out in England around 1500 – except perhaps in the wildest parts of the Peak District. In Scotland it was probably in the eighteenth century, although one was reported in 1888. But reports of wolves have continued long past these dates. Could they be true or are they wishful thinking?

One of my own most magical animal experiences was (almost) meeting a wild wolf in a forest in Central Europe. It was high summer and my wife, Sue, and I had stopped for a picnic in a glade halfway up a mountain. Suddenly everything seemed to go quiet and across the glade behind Sue strolled a wolf – out of the trees, across a few yards of open grass, and then it disappeared again. It did not look our way, although I am sure it knew we were there. It just walked by, minding its own business, almost as if we were not worthy of its notice. Sue knew nothing about it until later when I told her. People have suggested that it was a dog, but wolves and dogs look and move very differently, as you will know from all those films where they use German Shepherds as very poor stand-ins for wolves!

How Wolf Lost His Tail

One day Wolf and Fox were out together taking a look around and searching for an easy supply of food. They found a farm where someone had placed a dish of porridge on a window-sill to cool, so without a moment's hesitation, they knocked it down and lapped it up. Wolf was by far the larger of the two animals and had long legs and sharp teeth so he ate most of it and Fox was left to lick out the bowl. Fox resented this and decided he'd get his own back.

A few weeks later they were out together again. It was a cold, icy day and the sun was going down. Up in the deep-blue sky the full moon could clearly be seen and Fox saw it reflecting in the ice in the farmyard pond. This was his chance. 'I smell cheese,' he said, 'and look, there it is.'

'But how will we get it?' asked Wolf, 'It's very near the farmhouse.'

'You wait here,' said Fox, 'I will scout round and see if it's all clear. If you sit on the cheese that will make sure no one else comes and sees it.'

So Wolf sat down on the cold ice and covered the 'cheese' with his long, bushy tail. Fox was gone a long time and the night got colder and colder and the ice froze thicker and thicker and Wolf's tail froze to the ice on the pond where the 'cheese' had been.

When he thought enough time had passed, Fox ran to the farmhouse and quietly woke the farmer. 'Come quick,' he whispered, 'the Wolf is in the farmyard and he'll eat all your chickens. He might even eat up your children!'

The farmer and all his men came out with sticks and pitch-forks, shouting and making such a noise that Wolf, who had been half asleep, almost jumped right out of his skin. Luckily for him he didn't, but when he jumped up to run off he did leave most of his tail stuck in the ice.

And that's why, now, Wolf's tail is nowhere near as grand as Fox's brush.

THE WOLF OF ALLENDALE

It was just before Christmas in the year 1904 and the sheep farmers around the Northumberland village of Allendale had taken to stabling their flocks every night to try to prevent the losses they had been suffering for the past few weeks. Several dead sheep had been found and they were obviously the kills of a large predator. All that was found of one ewe was the head and horns. Other sheep that survived the attacks had wounds around their necks and on their legs.

Then a culprit was found – a wolf had escaped from the estate of Captain Baine of Shotley Bridge. But it was found that Baine's wolf was a cub, only four and a half months old, so not capable of doing much damage. It probably hadn't survived for very long by itself, so it couldn't be the guilty animal.

Everyone was talking about the wolf and gradually reports began to filter in: someone had spotted it in a field; someone else had found tracks; a den had been found … and then a large, imposing grey wolf was seen near Allenheads School. That was dangerous. The people feared for their children. Wolves rarely attack adults but a small child might be a different matter.

Hunting parties were assembled, growing larger each day; 100 men, 200 men, with dogs and guns. Rewards were offered. Famous hunting and tracking dogs were enlisted. Big game hunters arrived to prove their prowess. But no wolves were found, or even positively identified. The whole thing began to take on the atmosphere of a folkloric ritual – hunt days were holidays, people came in fancy dress, toasts were drunk and songs were sung!

Over the next few weeks the wolf was reported several times. People had seen it in a field or jumping over a wall. Every description was different as regards size and colour. More dead sheep were found. Could there be a whole pack of wolves working in the district?

In January the body of a dead wolf was found on the railway tracks at Cumwinton near Carlisle – not too far away. The local papers denied that it was the Wolf of Allendale and the Wolf

Committee were certain that the Allendale pack was still active. In some way, they wanted it to be. But then, as the months went by, interest waned; there were no more kills, no more sightings, no more dead wolves were found.

The whole story gradually faded from interest. Had it been just that, a story? Or was there a Wolf of Allendale?

Werewolves

The 'Wolf of Allendale' seems to be the straightforward tale of a real animal – a wolf, or perhaps a dog, attacking flocks. But there are some stories about wolves that don't seem to be quite 'natural'.

The Black Dog of the Wild Forest was a pretty frightening beast. A wolf could be even more frightening, but worst of all must be a werewolf. Werewolves are supposed to be people infected with a 'disease' which makes them turn into a wolf when there is a full moon. (There are also werefoxes, werecats and all kinds of other strange beasts!) They then go hunting for flesh, preferably human. Anyone who gets bitten, but not killed, catches the disease and, in turn, becomes a werewolf themselves. Historically, werewolves have been a European phenomenon: in France, Germany, Bohemia and so on, rather than British. They've become very popular in Britain and America in recent years though, particularly amongst young people.

Our stories are far older, but before you read them we have a decision to make: we have to decide whether a werewolf is animal or human. If it is 100 per cent human then it doesn't belong in this book; if it is even partly animal it does. I have come to the conclusion that, for most of the time, the person afflicted with lycanthropy is a normal human being but with an animal's instincts lurking just below the surface. However, at full moon, or when stimulated in some other way, he or she becomes completely an animal, but is more dangerous than most animals because the creature also has the guile and intelligence of a human being. So we will allow it …

AN ALMOST HUMAN BEAST

It was just after dusk and there was a full moon down near the horizon, a strange blood-red moon. People saw it and were frightened. They thought it was a sign that something evil was at large. The inns and drinking houses were full of people talking and speculating as to what it might mean. On the road from Denbigh to Wrexham a stagecoach was making its way along as fast as the two horses could manage. Suddenly, an enormous black creature, almost as long as one of the coach horses, appeared from nowhere and leapt at the coach causing the horses to shy and the coach to overturn. The beast then started to devour one of the horses while the other broke free and galloped off in panic. This was in the winter of 1790.

A few months later, in early 1791, a farmer went into one of his fields and in the snow saw prints that looked like those of an enormous wolf. He called on the blacksmith to accompany him and they followed the trail for about two miles to a neighbouring farm, where they came upon a scene of horror. The trail led them to a snow-covered field which was like a lake of blood, dotted with the carcasses of sheep and cattle. There was also the body of a farm dog.

They went to the farmhouse and found it locked and barricaded. They banged and called and eventually managed to persuade the terrified farmer to open the door and let them in. He told them that he had heard a sound in the yard and when he went to investigate he saw a huge, wolf-like animal ripping

the throat out of his dog. When the creature saw the farmer it went for him, but he managed to escape into the house and bolt the door. He hid under the table while the creature banged on the door, almost as a man would. It banged so hard that he was afraid it would knock it off its hinges. Then the most frightening thing of all happened: the creature rose on to its hind legs and peered in through the window. Its eyes were blue and it looked intelligent and human.

All the local people gathered at the church and prayers were said, before groups armed with guns and pitchforks went out to hunt for the beast. Nothing was ever found, apart from more tracks.

THE DERBYSHIRE WEREWOLF

In the far north-west of Derbyshire, on the borders with what is now Greater Manchester but was Lancashire and Cheshire, the Monk's Road runs through Longdendale. It was built by the monks of Basingwerk to travel between that town and their abbey near Holywell in North Wales. Somewhere along that road there used to be a large stone called the Abbot's Chair on which the Abbot of Basingwerk sometimes sat to hold court – to hear the complaints of his people, to dispense justice and to collect tithes and rents.

Long ago, in the reign of King Henry II, the abbot was doing just that. Towards the middle of the day there appeared before him a poor old woman. She was supporting herself on a stick and sobbing and was almost unable to walk with misery. She told the abbot that she had an enemy who was making her life unbearable and she had no idea what she'd done to deserve it. Through witchcraft, this woman – this enemy – had already brought about the death of the old woman's husband and her children; her cattle had all died; her crops had failed and now she had no way of supporting herself. She was penniless, had no way of feeding herself and feared that she too would soon be dead.

When the abbot asked if there was any way for other authorities to catch and punish this woman, she told him that the witch had the power of changing shape – of appearing as either a woman or a man, or of becoming any animal or bird she wished, so it was impossible to catch her or to prove that it was she who had done the deed.

On hearing this, the abbot was furious. First he helped the old woman in a practical way by giving her a sum of money to enable her to pay her rent and feed herself for the near future, and then he turned his thoughts towards the witch. He spoke a dreadful curse, 'May the hand of Heaven fall upon this wicked mortal and, in whatever shape she be at the present moment, may that shape cling to her until justice be done.'

Now, that morning the old witch had changed herself into the shape of a wolf and in that shape had slaughtered several sheep in neighbouring villages. At the moment the abbot proclaimed his curse, still in wolf shape, she was sleeping off her dinner of prime mutton under a bramble bush.

By coincidence, good King Henry himself was also in the Longdendale Forest. As the guest of the Baron of Ashton-under-Lyne he was indulging himself with hunting in the company of other local noblemen, his son, Prince Henry, and the Lord of Longdendale. The hunting was good as the forests around there were full of deer and boasted some of the largest wild boar in the country, as well as wolves and all kinds of smaller game. The Lord of Longdendale had made the most prestigious kill so far that day, bagging several ferocious wild cats which they called 'British tigers'. The young, proud Prince Henry was eager to outdo him, so he slipped off unaccompanied into a remote part of the forest away from the din of the hunting party where, he hoped, he could find some worthy prey.

And he was not disappointed.

Prince Henry was suddenly set upon by a ferocious wolf. It charged from the undergrowth in a furious attack and the surprise and the speed of the onslaught nearly dismounted the prince. Luckily his horse took avoiding action and enabled the prince to stab at the beast with his hunting spear. He felt the point enter the wolf's side and as it did so the beast emitted an almost human cry. Then the wolf rose up on its hind legs, took the spear in its forepaws and with its jaws snapped it in half as if it was a twig. The prince drew his sword, but the beast leapt at him and knocked him from his horse before he was able to use it. They grappled on the ground, the wolf trying for the prince's throat and the prince attempting to strangle the wolf. Over and over they thrashed and the prince's strength was rapidly fading.

His life was saved in the nick of time by the Baron of Ashton, who appeared on the scene having been sent to find him when he was missed from the main party. The baron, coming up behind, slew the wolf and rescued the prince. Then the baron escorted the prince back to the main party and they all returned to the baron's castle. The carcass of the wolf was also taken there, along with the other game they had killed that day.

After dinner, King Henry rewarded the baron for saving the life of his son and then, with great ceremony, the huge wolf carcass was slit open and out of its stomach rolled the heads of three young children whom it had taken as a tasty snack before finding the sheep. Everyone was amazed as wolves rarely attack people, preferring to slink around the outskirts of their farms taking far easier prey in the shape of young or injured livestock. Everyone remarked on how unusual this wolf was and the prince spoke about its amazing ferocity and boldness. He also told of how its cries had often sounded almost human in tone.

Then a forester spoke up and said that he had a story to tell which might cast light on the mystery. Around midday, he said, he had been hiding in ambush in the forest, hoping to catch a gang of poachers who were ignoring the forest laws and taking game for their own tables, when he was startled by a thrashing in some nearby bushes. Out of them came a large wolf who seemed to be trying to scramble out of its own skin, in much the same way as a man scrambles out of his clothes. The wolf was making sounds which almost sounded like the enraged cries of an old woman. It was very unusual behaviour for a wolf, said the forester. He had seen hundreds of wolves but had never seen or heard one like that.

While the forester was telling his tale the Abbot of Basingwerk arrived to pay homage to the king and when he heard the story he was able to tell of his encounter that morning with the poor old woman and of his curse on the witch.

And so it became clear that the wolf killed by the Baron of Ashton-under-Lyne was the old witch, trapped in her werewolf shape by the abbot's curse. Justice had been done far more quickly than he could ever have imagined.

REYNARDINE

'Reynardine' is a British ballad which first appeared in the eighteenth century as 'The Mountains High'. By the following century it could be found on both sides of the Atlantic. In those early versions there was no suggestion of the supernatural, it was simply a song about a robber or highwayman. The magical element seems to have been added, or brought out, by the singer and folklorist A.L. Lloyd in the 1960s.

Lloyd was well known for rewriting traditional material. He took the hero's name, originally some variant of 'Rinordine' or 'Ranordine', and by changing it to look like the French word for fox – *renard* – and accentuating a single line – 'his teeth so bright did shine' – he transformed the robber into a werewolf (or werefox, perhaps). A moment of inspiration!

I have sung 'Reynardine' for the last twenty years or so, having originally learned it to perform with the group, Popeluc. Popeluc were a trio made up of Ioan Pop, from Maramures in Romania; my daughter, Lucy Castle, who was studying traditional fiddle styles in Romania for a PhD; and myself. Originally we set out to play Popica's music to a British audience in as authentic a way as possible, but we soon expanded that brief to include playing British music with Romanian influences, and vice versa.

All most people knew about Romania (and particularly Transylvania) at that time was Dracula(!), so 'Reynardine', with its hints of vampirism, was ideal material and I am very proud of the version we recorded on the CD, *Blue Dor*. It is a great song and I always picture it happening on the East Cliff at Whitby!

One evening as I rambled amongst the springing thyme
I overhead a young woman converse with Reynardine.
Her hair was black, her skin was white and her lips as red as wine
And he smiled to gaze upon her, did that sly, bold Reynardine.

She said, 'Young man be civil and my company forsake
For it is my good opinion, I think you are a rake.'
He said, 'My dear, I am no rake brought up in Venus' train
But I'm seeking for concealment from the judge's men.'

Her cherry cheek, her ruby lips, they lost their former dye
And she fell into his arms amongst the mountains high.
He hadn't kissed her once or twice 'til she came to again
And modestly she asked him, 'Pray, sir, what's your name?'

He said, 'If by chance you ask of me perhaps you'll not me find
But I'll be in my castle, enquire for Reynardine.'
Day and night she followed him, his teeth so bright did shine,
And he led her o'er the mountain, did that brave, bold Reynardine.

Old Daddy Fox

We've now moved from dogs to wolves to foxes. People's attitudes towards foxes are very varied. To some they are vermin and need to be wiped off the face of the earth, to some they are sport to be chased and hunted, to others they are beautiful, clever animals. So, foxes: clever, wily heroes or villains?

CHANTICLEER AND PERTELOTE

This tale was used by Chaucer as the 'Nun's Priest's Tale' in The Canterbury Tales, *but it had probably been around for centuries even then.*

There was a woman, a widow, who lived in a cottage down a lane, near a wood. This woman had two daughters and she kept the three of them through hard work and by being careful. They didn't get ill through overeating because they lived very frugally on the food they could produce themselves, and they never suffered from drinking too much because all they drank was water from the well or milk fresh from the cow.

On her small piece of land the woman kept three cows, three pigs and a sheep called Moll. She also had a cock and some hens who provided her with a good supply of eggs. This cock was a rooster called Chanticleer and he was a magnificent bird. On his head he had a comb as red as coral, his legs and feet were of azure with sharp white spurs, his beak was as black as the darkest night and the rest of his plumage was as gold as the sun.

But his magnificence didn't lay just in his looks, Chanticleer was famous for his crowing. Every morning, just before the sun poked the first fingers of light over the horizon, Chanticleer would be waiting on his perch ready to greet the new day with the loudest, finest clarion call. None of the other cocks in the neighbourhood would dare raise a sound until Chanticleer had heralded the day.

Chanticleer had a harem of nine fine hens, all coloured like himself – but not so magnificently – and of these, his favourite was Pertelote. Pertelote roosted beside him on the topmost perch and was always the wife he mated with first when he felt the urge come over him. She was his wife, his help and his confidante.

And then, one morning, the unthinkable happened. Dawn began to spread across the sky but Chanticleer hadn't crowed. Pertelote, on the perch beside him, gave him a nudge. Chanticleer took a breath and stretched his neck but, instead of greeting the morning with a great crow of joy, the only sound to come from his throat was a sigh. Such a sigh as you've never heard!

Pertelote was beside herself. She couldn't believe it. What was wrong with her husband? What would happen if he didn't crow? She nudged him again and told him he mustn't wait a moment longer, she encouraged him and cajoled him and, in the end, realised that something must be really wrong. 'I can't crow,' he said. 'My life is over. I have seen it in a dream. My end has come.'

'A dream?' squawked Pertelote. 'You've had a dream? We all have dreams! Dreams mean nothing, you just ate too much too late last night. I don't want a husband who is frightened by dreams!'

But Chanticleer insisted that this was not just an ordinary dream. It was an omen, a sign, and he told her about it. 'I dreamed I was in the yard,' he said, 'and things were just as usual, but then I saw something in the long grass by the ditch. It was like a dog, but it wasn't a dog. Its colour was red and its tail had a black tip; its ears were pointed and its nose was long and sharp – but not as sharp as its teeth! Oh, those teeth! It was terrible and it was there to eat me!' So lamented poor Chanticleer.

Again Pertelote told him not to be a fool. No hen wanted a husband who was a coward. Scared of a dream indeed! Then Chanticleer spoke about the long history of dreams and of all the people they knew who had had dreams which turned out to be true, and then he went on to famous people: he spoke of Joseph in the Bible and how he had dreamed the Plagues of Egypt, and he quoted Daniel and Croesus and Hector's wife. They had all had dreams that foretold events that had then happened.

Chanticleer went on and on in great detail and you might think this would have made him even more afraid, but it had the opposite effect. Suddenly he pulled himself together. He sat up on his perch, stretched his neck skyward and let fly his usual welcome to the morning. All the other cocks joined in, glad that things were back to normal. Then Chanticleer led the hens into the yard where he mounted them all several times, as he had done when he was young and full of life, and they scratched and pecked all around.

After a while Chanticleer's attention was caught by a butterfly which fluttered past him and into the grass by the ditch. He watched it and then looked, and looked again. There, nearly hidden by the long grass, was the tormentor from his dreams. It lay still, watching him. 'Don't be afraid,' it said. 'I haven't come to harm you. In fact, just the opposite. I am a great aficionado

of music and, wherever I have been, I have heard tell of your crowing. I have heard that you have the loudest, most magnificent voice in the land, and I just had to come to hear it for myself. Please, good cock, let me hear so that I can judge if it really is as good as they say.'

Now flattery will get you everywhere, so Chanticleer forgot all about his dream and drew himself up to his full height, took a deep breath, stood on tiptoe, stretched his neck ... and, as swift as lightning, the fox grabbed him, threw him up on its back, and squeezed through a hole in the hedge and was gone. Pertelote and the other hens set up such a commotion that the old woman and her daughters came out to see what was happening. They were just in time to see the back of the fox disappearing from sight, and they shouted and screamed and ran after him banging pans and waving their broomsticks. The fox ran across the field and into the wood followed by the women and some men from the village with their dogs, and the cows, and not forgetting Moll the sheep and a flock of hissing geese and a swarm of bees ...

When he reached the safety of the wood the fox lay down to recover his breath. The hue and cry was in the distance but here he felt safe – for a while. Then Chanticleer, who had got over the shock of being taken, spoke. 'You are safe for a minute,' he said, 'but pretty soon those men and their dogs are going to find you and they'll catch you and kill you. If I were you, I'd call out and say "Be off with you, I'm going to eat this cock whatever you do, but if you don't let me eat it in peace a terrible pestilence will fall upon you. So be off!"'

The fox, thinking this was a good plan, opened his mouth to call out and no sooner had he done so than Chanticleer wriggled free and flapped up into the branches of a tree. But the fox wasn't finished. 'I think we have misunderstood each other,' he said.

'I wasn't telling stories, I really do want to hear your crow. I only brought you out here so that I could have you all to myself and I could listen without the noise of those silly chatterbox hens.'

'Be quiet,' said Chanticleer. 'I was a fool to let myself be caught once but I'd be more than a fool if I fell for the same trick a second time!'

And the fox, seeing that he was beaten, slunk off to try his luck somewhere else.

And that is the end of the story of Chanticleer and Pertelote. You might think it is just a silly story about a cock, a hen and a fox, but if you do then I suggest you read it again and think what you might be able to learn from it. (At least, that is what Chaucer suggested.)

THE FOX AND THE COCK

One day, a fox met a cock and they began talking. 'How many tricks can you do?' asked the fox.

'Well,' said the cock, 'I think I could probably do three; how many can you do?'

'I can do three score and thirteen!' boasted the fox.

'What tricks are they then?' asked the cock. 'Will you show me?'

'Well,' said the fox, 'there's one I learned from my grandfather … he used to shut one eye and give a great, loud shout.'

'Oh, that's nothing. I could do that myself,' said the cock.

'Go on then, do it,' said the fox. So the cock shut one eye and crowed as loud as ever he could. But he shut the eye that was next to the fox and the fox grabbed him by the neck and ran away with him.

The cock's wife, the chicken to whom he belonged, saw what was happening and cried out, 'Let go of that cock; he's mine.'

The cock shuddered. 'Oh I think I'd rather you ran off with me than make me go back to her! Tell her "*Se mo choileach fhein a th' ann*" [It is my own cock],' said the cock to the fox (for he was an Irish cock!)

When the fox opened his mouth to say what the cock had told him to say the cock sprang from his jaws and up on to the roof of a house. There, he shut one eye again and gave a loud crow of victory; and that's the end of that tale.

THE FOX AND THE BAGPIPES

One day a hungry fox found a set of bagpipes which someone had dropped by the road. Now, today, the bags of bagpipes are probably made of all kinds of artificial high-tech materials, but in those times they were made of hide. The fox started to chew on the bag, for he was hungry, but there was still a tiny remnant of breath in it, so when the fox bit it the drone gave a groan. The fox, surprised but not frightened, said, 'Why, here I've found both meat and music!'

OLD DADDY FOX

I just had to include a version of this song. It's one of the best-known English language folk songs there is. Back when I was growing up a version sung by Burl Ives was regularly on children's radio programmes; more recently it has been recorded by people as unexpected as Bob Dylan and Bruce Springsteen! Everybody on the English folk club scene seems to have sung a version. This is the one I've sung for at least three decades. I can't remember where I learned it from.

Old Daddy Fox went out on a wintry night
He called to the moon to afford him light
For he had many long miles to travel that night
Before he reached that town-O, town-O, town-O,
He had many long miles to travel that night
Before he reached that town-O.

At first he came to the farmer's yard
Where the ducks and the geese declared it hard
That their nerves should be shattered and their rest be marred
By the visit of Mr Fox-O, Fox-O, Fox-O,
That their nerves should be shattered and their rest be marred
By the visit of Mr Fox-O.

He grabbed the old grey goose by the sleeve
Said he, 'Madam Goose, and by your leave
I'll carry you away without reprieve
And take you home to my den-O, den-O, den-O,
I'll carry you away without reprieve
And take you home to my den-O.'

He seized the black duck by the neck
And slung her up all on his back
The black duck cried out, 'Quack, quack, quack.'
With her legs hanging dangling down-O, down-O, down-O,
The black duck cried out, 'Quack, quack, quack.'
With her legs hanging dangling down-O.

Old Mother Wigger-Wagger jumped out of bed,
Out of the window she popped her old head
She said, 'John, John, the black duck's gone
And the fox is off to his den-O, den-O, den-O,
John, John, the black duck's gone
And the fox is off to his den-O.'

Then John went up on to the hill
And he blew a blast both loud and shrill
Said the Fox, 'That's pretty fine music, still
I'd rather be home in my den-O, den-O, den-O.'
Said the Fox, 'That's pretty fine music, still
I'd rather be home in my den-O.'

At last the fox came to his den
There sat the little ones 8, 9, 10
Said he, 'You're in luck, here's a big fat duck
With her legs hanging dangling down-O, down-O, down-O.'
Said he, 'You're in luck, here's a big fat duck
With her legs hanging dangling down-O.'

He then sat down with his hungry wife
And they did very well without a fork or a knife
And he never ate a better duck in all his life
And the little ones chewed on the bones-O, bones-O, bones-O,

He never ate a better duck in all his life
And the little ones chewed on the bones-O.

THE FOX AND THE PIXIES

*This story was collected on Dartmoor in the 1860s. It's a variation
of a very well-known tale. The 1860 version didn't really have an
ending – it just stopped – so I made one based on a few suggestions
given to me by a little pig …*

One night, Mr Fox went out on the prowl but could find
no prey. He went all around the fields and hedges which were
his regular hunting grounds, but there was nothing, so he went
further afield. He followed tracks and ditches and crossed fields
and woods until he found himself in countryside which was
new to him, and there he found a little cluster of houses in
which the pixies lived.

Now Mr Fox loved eating rabbits and birds but even better
were the farmer's hens, and even better than hens were pixies!
So Mr Fox went up to the first pixie house, which was made of
wood, and knocked on the door. 'Let me in, let me in!' he called.

'I won't, and you can't come in because the door is locked,'
squeaked the frightened pixie in the wooden house.

Mr Fox climbed up on to the roof of the house and jumped
up and down and rocked about until the wooden walls collapsed and the roof fell in and he was able to eat up the pixie.

Then Mr Fox went over to the next house, which was made
of stone. 'Let me in, let me in!' he called.

'I won't, and you can't come in because the door is locked,'
squeaked the frightened pixie in the stone house.

Again Mr Fox climbed up on to the roof of the house and
jumped up and down and rocked about until some of the stones

at the bottom of the stone walls rolled away and the walls collapsed and the roof fell in and he was able to eat up the pixie.

Then he went to the third house, which was made of iron. 'Let me in, let me in!' he called.

'I won't, and you can't come in because the door is locked,' squeaked the frightened pixie in the iron house.

'But I bring you good news,' whispered Mr Fox.

'I know what you want,' replied the pixie, 'and I know what you've done to my friends. You're not coming in here.'

So once again Mr Fox climbed up on to the roof of the house and jumped up and down and rocked about and stamped his feet and did everything he could think of to bring the house down, but the iron house was too strong even for Mr Fox and, in the end, he had to go away.

But next evening he came back and tried every trick he knew to persuade the pixie to open the door and let him in, but the pixie wasn't interested … until Mr Fox mentioned a field of turnips which he knew of, not too far away. The pixie liked turnips, so Mr Fox offered to take the pixie and show him where it was. They agreed to meet at four o'clock the next morning, just before it got light.

Mr Fox thought he was pretty clever coming up with this plan, but unfortunately for him the pixie was even cleverer. He'd got enough clues from Mr Fox to be able to work out where the turnip field was and by the time Mr Fox arrived at his house at four o'clock he'd been to the turnip field, collected all the turnips he wanted, and was locked safely back in his iron house.

Mr Fox was stumped, he couldn't think of another plan to catch the pixie for a long time, until he remembered that there was going to be a fair in the neighbouring town. It was a famous fair to which everyone went, so he suggested to the pixie that they should go together. The pixie didn't trust Mr Fox and I don't blame him, but Mr Fox apologised and said he was truly sorry for trying to eat him before, and he wouldn't ever do it again, and he regretted eating the pixie's neighbours, and now they should all start again and be friends, and what better way was there to mark this than the pixie allowing Mr Fox to take him to the fair and to treat him to a really good day out?

In the end the pixie agreed, and they arranged to set off early the next morning. But again, the pixie was too clever for Mr Fox. He'd been to the fair and was on his way home again with his fairings when Mr Fox approached his house. He'd bought a crock, a clock and a frying pan. When he saw Mr Fox, the pixie climbed into the crock and rolled down the hill and was safely home before Mr Fox realised what was happening.

The next day Mr Fox arrived at the iron house again. By now he was so angry at being made a fool of by the pixie that he was not thinking straight. He was desperate to catch the pixie and was willing to try anything to do so. As he stood outside the front door he heard a new sound, a regular sort of beating, ticking sound which he didn't recognise.

'I know what it is,' he thought to himself, 'it's his heartbeat. Now where is it coming from?' Mr Fox listened hard and turned his head this way and that. He walked round and round the house, listening as he did so, and decided that the noise was coming from up on the roof. 'He's up there,' he thought, 'I've got him. He's trapped.'

Mr Fox scrambled up on to the roof and near the chimney he saw a face. As he reached out for it there was a sudden, deafening ringing of bells and the face leapt in the air and wobbled from side to side. Mr Fox was so alarmed that he slipped and fell down the chimney, straight into a frying pan full of hot oil which was waiting below.

And Mr Fox never bothered that pixie, or anyone else, again.

Scrapefoot

Once upon a time there were three bears who lived in a big house in the middle of a forest. One was a huge bear, one was a middling sort of bear, and the other was a very small bear. In the same forest lived a wily little fox called Scrapefoot. Scrapefoot was clever, but he was also nosy and inquisitive and sometimes that got him into trouble!

Scrapefoot was afraid of the three bears but, in a strange way, he was also fascinated by them and wanted to find out more about them. He spent a lot of his time watching them and listening to them – but always from a safe hiding place. He would have loved to be able to sneak into their house and have a look around but he didn't think he'd ever get the chance … or be brave enough if he did.

And then, one day, he happened to be near the bears' house when he caught a glimpse of their three backsides disappearing into the trees. At least he thought it was their three backsides. He was pretty sure there was a huge backside and probably a middling sort of backside, but he wasn't so sure about a very small backside, although there might have been.

So Scrapefoot tiptoed up to the door of the grand house and carefully tried the handle. It turned and the door opened. Scrapefoot quietly peered in and listened very carefully. The house had that unmistakeable sound of a place that's empty – a sound which is more than silence. He must have seen all three bears going out, the small one must have been there too. He put one paw in, and listened. Then he put another paw in, and listened again. And then he crept into the house and started to look around.

He went across the hall and opened the first door. It was a sitting room and there were three chairs – a huge chair, a middling sort of chair and a very small chair. Scrapefoot jumped up

on to the huge chair and looked around, but the chair was so huge and high that it made his back hurt and he felt dizzy, so he jumped down and climbed on to the middling sort of chair. It was better, but however much he turned himself around and shuffled about he couldn't get really comfortable. So Scrapefoot got off the middling sort of chair and sat down on the very small chair. It was a perfect fit but, as he relaxed into it, it suddenly broke to pieces under him.

Scrapefoot was shocked but otherwise unhurt so he climbed up off the floor. Then he stood still and listened. Had the noise of his fall summoned anyone to see what was happening? No, all was quiet, so he started to look round the room a bit more. On the table were three cups. He jumped up to have a look and see if there was anything to drink in them. They were all full of milk. Scrapefoot tasted the milk in the huge cup, but it was sour so he only had a sip and then moved on to the middling sort of cup. The milk in that was better but he still didn't really like it, so he tried the milk in the very small cup and it was so delicious that he drank it all up.

Now Scrapefoot thought he'd go and look around the rest of the house. He tiptoed up the stairs and found a bedroom in which were three beds – a huge bed, a middling sort of bed and a very small bed. Scrapefoot jumped up on to the huge bed and laid down, but the bed was hard and lumpy and he wouldn't have wanted to sleep there, so he jumped down and climbed on to the middling sort of bed. It was too soft and the pillows were so deep that he couldn't see anything, or even breathe very well. Scrapefoot got off the middling sort of bed and lay down on the very small bed. It was a perfect fit and so comfortable that he fell straight to sleep.

I don't know how long Scrapefoot slept but he was woken by noises downstairs. A huge voice said, 'Who's been sitting in my chair?' and straight away it was answered by a middling sort of voice, which asked, 'Who's been sitting in my chair?' And then there was a wail and a very small voice sobbed, 'Who's been sitting in my chair … and has broken it to pieces?'

And then a huge voice said, 'Who's been drinking my milk?' and straight away it was answered by a middling sort of voice, which asked, 'Who's been drinking my milk?' And then there was another wail and a very small voice sobbed, 'Who's been drinking my milk … and hasn't left any for me?'

And then Scrapefoot heard the sound of footsteps on the stairs. It was too late to escape and he was too terrified to run away, so he lay still in the very small bed. The three bears came into the bedroom and a huge voice said, 'Who's been sleeping in my bed?' and straight away it was answered by a middling sort of voice, which asked, 'Who's been sleeping in my bed?'

And then there was a wail and a very small voice sobbed, 'Who's been sleeping in my bed … and he's still there!'

The three bears came and stood around the bed and looked at Scrapefoot. 'What shall we do with him?' they wondered.

'Let's hang him,' said the huge bear.

'Let's drown him,' said the middling-sized bear.

'Let's throw him out of the window,' said the very small bear.

And the three bears picked up Scrapefoot and they swung him backwards and forwards and backwards and forwards and threw him out of the window. As he flew through the air Scrapefoot thought he was certain to be killed, but luckily he landed in a nice, soft bush and wasn't hurt so very badly at all. He picked himself up and stretched each leg in turn – they weren't broken – and he wagged his tail – that was OK, just a bit bent – and then he ran off home as fast as he could go.

When he arrived safely at home Scrapefoot vowed that he wouldn't go near the bears' house again. And he didn't. If he saw the bears while he was out and about on his business he would quickly and silently creep away and find somewhere safe to hide until they had gone away.

Everybody knows the famous story of 'Goldilocks and the Three Bears', as told by the poet, Southey, either from books or films or TV retellings. There is an earlier version, in which the young Goldilocks is an old, silver-haired woman, and Joseph Jacobs himself suggested that Scrapefoot was the original from which Southey drew his inspiration.

4

A GAME OF CAT AND MOUSE

ALIEN BIG CATS

At this point I would love to tell you a tale about an alien big cat (an ABC, as fans of the paranormal call them) or even of a real, solid, big cat living in the British countryside, but I can't. Because there aren't any really (stories I mean, not cats, although perhaps I mean that as well). There are little snippets, little anecdotes, tall tales men will tell in the pub or on a website – there are hundreds of websites devoted to them. There are beliefs.

Thousands, possibly millions, of people believe that there are wild cats living in Britain. Some people think they are leopards or pumas, even lions or tigers. Some think they are a native wild cat, so far unknown to science. Pawmarks have been photographed, as have dead animals, there are a few grainy bits of film or video, some of which are definitely fakes and others just film of ordinary moggies, and the rest can't be proved or disproved. Every now and again there is a hue and cry and packs of hunters and dogs and film crews set out to catch, say, the 'Beast of Bodmin', but so far no one has! In a way, these cats seem to have taken over from the Loch Ness monster.

Strangely, there were no reports of large, wild cats before the middle of the twentieth century ... except for one.

In the 1770s the famous radical writer William Cobbett described a hollow tree at Waverly, near Farnham, where:

> I, when a very little boy, once saw a cat go, that was as big as a
> middle sized spaniel dog ... [Many years later] in New Brunswick
> I saw the great wild grey cat which is there called a Lucifee; and it
> seemed to me just such a cat as I had seen at Waverley.

A 'Lucifee' is a lynx, so did the young Cobbett see a wild lynx in Surrey? We'll never know. If he did, it was probably an escapee from a collection, like the Bengal tigers mentioned elsewhere. But we must not forget the 'ferocious wild cats which they called British tigers' which were mentioned in 'The Derbyshire Werewolf' story. I wonder what they were ...

Place names can sometimes give us clues. There are many places in Britain with 'cat' as part of the name, but most of those are derived from Old English or Scandinavian personal names like Catta or Kati. Others derive from the Celtic/British word *cadeir*, which literally means 'a chair' and was used of high places (like Arthur's Seat in Edinburgh). But there are some which seem to mean a place frequented by cats: there is Catfield in Norfolk (open land frequented by cats); Catford, London, and Carforth, Lancashire (a ford frequented by wild cats); Catmore, Berkshire (a pool or mere frequented by wild cats); Catmose, Rutland (a marsh frequented by wild cats) and so on, including Catsfield, Catshill, Cattal, Cattawade, Cattishall, Catton ...

Surely these wouldn't have been just feral moggies? To warrant having a place named after them they must have been impressive and perhaps even dangerous.

The Scottish wild cat used to be found all over Britain and that is very fierce when cornered, although they try to avoid people if they can. There are tales of them 'hanging from tree branches by a hook at the end of their tail, [and] dropping on to passing crofters and tearing out their throats'. That sounds fierce enough to name a place after! And recent archaeological finds have proved that lynxes were still in Britain at the time of the Anglo-Saxon settlement, so either of those might have suggested place names.

But are any of them still living here? Make up your own mind and, meanwhile, we'll have some stories about the more everyday sort of cat …

THE KING O' THE CATS

If dogs are 'man's best friend', I'm sure cats must run them a pretty close second. There are probably more cats around than dogs because they can, and often do, survive by themselves. I expect you've noticed that they have a very well-defined hierarchy and every cat knows its place. This very well-known and well-loved story is from Joseph Jacobs' More British Folk Tales, *and it is so well told that I have done very little to it.*

One winter's evening the sexton's wife was sitting by the fireside with her big black cat, Old Tom, on the other side of the fire, both half asleep and waiting for the master to come home. They waited and they waited, but still he didn't come, till at last he came rushing in, calling out, 'Who's Tommy Tildrum?' in such a wild way that both his wife and the cat stared at him to know what was the matter.

'Why, what's the matter?' said his wife. 'And why do you want to know who Tommy Tildrum is?'

'Oh, I've had such an adventure. I was digging away at old Mr Fordyce's grave when I suppose I must have dropped asleep, and only woke up when I heard a cat's meow.'

'Meow!' said Old Tom in answer.

'Yes, just like that! So I looked over the edge of the grave, and what do you think I saw?'

'Now, how can I tell?' asked the sexton's wife.

'Why, nine black cats all like our friend Tom here, all with a white spot on their chests. And what do you think they were carrying? Why, a small coffin covered with a black velvet pall, and on the pall was a small coronet all of gold, and at every third step they took they cried all together, "Meow".'

'Meow!' said Old Tom again.

'Yes, just like that!' said the sexton. 'And as they came nearer and nearer to me I could see them more distinctly, because their eyes shone out with a sort of green light. Well, they all came towards me, eight of them carrying the coffin and the biggest cat of all walking in front for all the world like … but look at our Tom, how he's looking at me. You'd think he knew all I was saying.'

'Go on, go on,' said his wife. 'Never mind Old Tom.'

'Well, as I was saying, they came towards me slowly and solemnly, and at every third step crying all together, "Meow".'

'Meow!' said Old Tom again.

'Yes, just like that, till they came and stood right opposite Mr Fordyce's grave, where I was. Then they all stood still and looked straight at me. I did feel queer, that I did! But look at Old Tom. He's looking at me just like they did.'

'Go on, go on,' said his wife. 'Never mind Old Tom.'

'Where was I? Oh, they all stood still looking at me and the one that wasn't carrying the coffin came forwards and, staring straight at me, said to me … yes, *said* to me … with a squeaky voice, "Tell Tom Tildrum that Tim Toldrum's dead", and that's why I asked you if you knew who Tom Tildrum is, for how can I tell Tom Tildrum Tim Toldrum's dead if I don't know who Tom Tildrum is?'

'Look at Old Tom! Look at Old Tom!' screamed his wife.

And well he might look, for Tom was swelling, and Tom was staring, and Tom was bristling, and at last Tom shrieked out, 'What? Old Tim dead! Then I'm the King o' the Cats!' and he rushed up the chimney and was never seen again.

WHY THE MANX CAT HAS NO TAIL

A Story of the Great Flood

You all know the story of how God decided to cleanse the earth by causing a Great Flood, and how he warned Noah about it and instructed him to build an ark and take into it two animals of every kind – male and female. Well, there were a few animals who didn't make it on to the ark – the unicorn for instance – and a few others who only just managed it by the skin of their teeth – or the tip of their tail in the case of the Manx cat!

The flood was rising rapidly and the ark was nearly full. Noah was preparing to close the doors. But at that moment the cat decided that she couldn't possibly go on such a long voyage without a mouse inside her. Once the voyage started she knew she wouldn't be allowed to eat either of the two mice on board, so she went mousing.

It was time to sail. Noah knew the cat was still missing, so he called and called. Still no cat. He started to close the door. He couldn't wait any longer. 'Oh well,' he thought, 'I did my best, but I don't know how the world will manage without cats …'

Just as he slammed the door shut, the cat, soaking wet and bedraggled but with a nice full stomach, scurried through the gap. The door slammed shut and sliced off the end of her tail. She didn't seem to mind, she just settled down to lick her lips and groom her wet fur. As she did so she purred:

'Bee bo, bend it,
My tail's ended,
I'll go to Man
Get copper nails
And mend it.'

But she never did and that is why, to this day, the Manx cat has no tail.

THE CHESHIRE CAT

My mind somehow associates the Manx cat with the Cheshire cat – if I think of one, the other comes to mind as well. They are probably equally well known but they are different categories of beast: a Manx cat is an actual flesh and blood creature, a Cheshire cat is not.

I thought the Cheshire cat was an invention of Lewis Carroll in *Alice's Adventures in Wonderland*, but that is not the case. True, that is where it makes its best-known appearance, with the iconic image by Sir John Tenniel of the body disappearing, leaving just the grin. But the saying 'Grinning like a Cheshire cat' pre-dates Alice by at least a century. A dictionary of 1788 includes the phrase and defines it as describing someone who shows their teeth and gums when they smile. Why? Well the people of Cheshire claim that their cows produce such fine milk that the farmyard cats there are always smiling. Well, that's their story and they're sticking to it!

THE CAT AND THE MOUSE

The cat and the mouse played in the malt-house.
The cat bit the mouse's tail off.
'Pray, puss, give me my tail,' begged the mouse.
'No,' said the cat, 'I'll not give you your tail; not till you go to the cow, and fetch me some milk.'
First she leapt, and then she ran,
Till she came to the cow, and thus began:

'Pray, cow, give me some milk, that I may give the cat milk, that the cat may give me my own tail again.'

'No,' said the cow, 'I will give you no milk; not till you go to the farmer and get me some hay.'

First she leapt, and then she ran.

Till she came to the farmer, and thus began:

'Pray, farmer, give me some hay, that I may give the cow hay, that the cow may give me milk, that I may give the cat milk, that the cat may give me my own tail again.'

'No,' says the farmer, 'I'll give you no hay; not till you go to the butcher and fetch me some meat.'

First she leapt, and then she ran.

Till she came to the butcher, and thus began:

'Pray, butcher, give me some meat, that I may give farmer meat, that the farmer may give me hay, that I may give the cow hay, that the cow may give me milk, that I may give the cat milk, that the cat may give me my own tail again.'

'No,' says the butcher, 'I'll give you no meat; not till you go to the baker and fetch me some bread.'

First she leapt, and then she ran.

Till she came to the baker, and thus began:

'Pray, baker, give me some bread, that I may give the butcher bread, that the butcher may give me meat, that I may give the farmer meat, that the farmer may give me hay, that I may give the cow hay, that the cow may give me milk, that I may give the cat milk, that the cat may give me my own tail again.'

'Yes,' says the baker, 'I'll give you some bread; but if you eat my meal, I'll cut off your head!'

Then the baker gave the mouse bread,
The mouse gave the butcher bread,

The butcher gave the mouse meat,

The mouse gave the farmer meat,

The farmer gave the mouse hay,

The mouse gave the cow hay,

The cow gave the mouse milk,

The mouse gave the cat milk,

and the cat gave the mouse her tail back again.

The Tale of Dick Whittington's Cat

This is not the historical tale of Sir Richard Whittington, merchant; nor is it the folk tale of Dick Whittington and his cat as portrayed in pantomimes. No, this is the tale of a young cat who happened to befriend a poor lad called Dick.

She was just an ordinary cat. She had been born in a shed, to a mother who wasn't exactly feral but who wasn't a house cat either. When she was old enough to fend for herself our cat made herself a living around the alleyways and yards in a part of London near the river. It was a mixed area with a lot of industry and trade and some very poor people, but there were also areas of good houses where prosperous people lived. This mix meant that life was good for an enterprising young cat. There were piles of litter to scavenge in, there were well-to-do people who would take her in and pet her for a while, there were kitchens where the cook would throw her titbits and, above all, there were plenty of rats and mice and she soon became an expert hunter.

One day, as she was patrolling her territory, she came upon a boy dozing under some steps. She wasn't hungry and had nothing else to do, so she rubbed round his rather tattered boots and he woke up and petted her. She liked him and stayed around him and they became good friends. The boy talked to her, or possibly to himself, as he fondled her ears and she learned that his name was Dick – Dick Whittington.

Dick was an orphan from Lancashire. His life there had been hard, cold and miserable, and he was unhappy. When he heard that in far-off London the streets were paved with gold and everyone lived a life of luxury, Dick set off to walk there. He reached London after many weeks, but far from being paved with gold, he found it a place of poverty and grime with the streets full of rubbish and running with excrement. The only work he could find was cleaning this mess off rich people's shoes. This enabled him to buy some poor food, but he still had nowhere to sleep, which is why the cat had found him dozing under the steps. His life was still hard, cold and miserable, and he was still unhappy, but that chance meeting turned out to be Dick's first piece of luck, and it was good for the cat as well.

Their second piece of luck came when Dick was taken in by a gentleman who found him sleeping in the street outside his house. This gentleman was called Mr Fitzwarren and he was a rich merchant. Mr Fitzwarren took pity on the boy and gave him a job running errands and a room to sleep in. The room was a garret in the roof and it was overrun with rats and mice, but Dick insisted on taking his friend the cat with him and within a few weeks there were no more vermin. Dick was able to settle down to a good sleep without being disturbed by their squeaking and without having them running all over his bed. Life improved for the rest of the family too.

Mr Fitzwarren traded with far-off lands. He bought and sold anything which he felt would raise a profit. He was a fair man and gave his employees a chance to profit in his expeditions too. He encouraged them to invest in the voyage by sending something which could be sold. Dick had nothing to send ... except for the cat. He didn't see how a cat could earn him money and he didn't want to part from his friend, but he sent it anyway.

So the cat was forced to leave her friend and make a new life on board ship. She didn't mind. There were plenty of rats and mice to eat and the crew fussed her and there were all kinds of new things to experience.

Then, one day, the ship was caught in a storm and driven ashore on the Barbary Coast of North Africa. The local ruler insisted on buying the entire cargo and invited all the crew to a banquet but, as soon as the food was served, before anyone had an opportunity to eat a single mouthful, a hoard of rats descended on it and ate every morsel.

The Moors explained that this happened all the time and they had no way of preventing it.

One of the sailors remembered the cat which had proved itself a good mouser on the voyage and had it brought ashore. It quickly set about the vermin and so impressed the ruler that he insisted on buying it for a lot of money. When he was told that it would soon have kittens he was even more pleased, as he would then have several cats to control the rats, so he paid more for the cat than for the rest of the cargo combined.

Because the cat had been Dick's investment all this money went to him. He became a gentleman and married Fitzwarren's daughter, Alice.

The cat lived on in the palace in North Africa and had many more litters of kittens, which thrived on the endless supply of rats and mice. And the rest, as they say, is history. Or, perhaps, just a folk tale.

Sir Richard Whittington (1354–1423) is a historical character who was three times Lord Mayor of London, a Member of Parliament and Sheriff of London. Although in reality his father was a knight (unlike in the pantomime where Dick is usually an orphan), Richard was a younger son so could not inherit the title and estate. Instead he became a very successful merchant. For some reason, he also became a character of folklore and pantomime.

Very little of the folk tale is true and even the fact that he had a cat is unproven, although there is a portrait of him with one on his lap (see illustration).

THE PIED PIPER OF FRANCHVILLE

This is not the pied piper you all know – the one from the German town of Hamelin which the Brothers Grimm and the poet Browning wrote about so famously. It couldn't be about him because this is a book of *British* stories. This is the Pied Piper of Newtown, or Franchville, as it was known in those days.

Today Newtown is a tiny hamlet, just a cluster of houses, on the north-west coast of the Isle of Wight. It is an important archaeological site, being a well-preserved medieval settlement. Newtown was originally called Franchville, or Freetown. By the fourteenth century it was the most important port on the island, but then something happened and it gradually fell into neglect until it became almost abandoned.

Historians will probably tell you that the change in the fortunes of Franchville was due to a combination of the plague and the harbour silting up. Because of the plague there were no young people about to maintain the harbour or to protect it when it was later attacked by the French. But was it the plague that removed all the young people? Or was it the Pied Piper?

Franchville was having trouble with rats. They were everywhere. There had always been *some* rats – there are in every seaport town – but recently their numbers had been increasing. Now they were out of control. You couldn't walk down the stairs without a rat tripping you up. Mothers couldn't go to bed at night but had to stay by their babies' cradles in case rats came and nibbled them. They didn't just nibble at the food in the larder, they ate every scrap of it, and it was not unusual for a housewife to stock up one day and then find an empty pantry the next.

When the trouble started, all the households in Franchville invested in cats. That worked for a while, but gradually the cats were outnumbered until even the most battle-hardened old fighters gave up and sneaked away. They tried poison, but if you're not very careful you finish up by poisoning yourself as well, and after that had happened a few times they dropped that idea. It was too dangerous.

And how about rat-catchers? Well, every rat-catcher from Land's End to John o'Groats came to Franchville at one time or another. They came with their traps and their poisons and their fierce little dogs and all kinds of fancy and magical ways of ridding the town of rats. But they all left after a while, knowing that this problem was beyond them.

The town council did not know what to do. They'd tried everything.

And then, one day, the Pied Piper arrived.

I don't know where he came from and no one else did either. He just appeared in the town, walking out of the sea-haze like the unknown rider in a spaghetti western. He pushed his way into the town hall and said softly, 'I hear you've got a problem.' And he offered to solve it in return for the sum of £50, which was a huge amount of money in those days. And the council agreed to pay it because they were so desperate, and they didn't think he could do it anyway.

The Pied Piper was a sight to behold – a very tall, very thin man with a bag on his back. And his clothing wasn't just pied (two-coloured), it contained just about every colour which had ever been dyed into material!

As soon as the bargain was struck the Pied Piper walked into the street, put his whistle to his lips and started to play a tune – a piercing, shrill, leaping tune, and from every nook and cranny of the town came a flood of leaping, shrieking rats. A tide of rats. There were so many of them that the streets turned black with a liquid wave of writhing bodies. The piper led the tumbling wave of rats up Silver Street into Gold Street and on towards the harbour. There, he climbed into a boat and, still playing away, sailed into the deep water in the middle of the harbour, where he stopped. The rats followed him into the sea and out to where he moored, and there they swam round and round the boat as the tide gradually went out. As the water disappeared the rats slowly sunk into the ooze, where they were stuck, and when the tide came back in they were all drowned.

Then the Pied Piper sailed to shore where he was greeted by the cheers of the townsfolk, who clapped and danced and set the church bells ringing. The only people who weren't delighted were the town council, for they did not have £50 in the town's coffers. As every politician that has ever lived will do, they tried to get out of the deal; they tried to bargain and beat the Pied Piper down. They said that anyone could have done what he had done so why should they pay him £50 for it?

The Pied Piper would have none of it. He insisted that he had a contract for £50, so it was £50 that they must pay. And he warned the council, 'That is not the only tune I can play … You would not want me to play the one I have in mind!'

'What? You have the impudence to threaten us, you strolling vagabond?' the mayor cried. 'Do your worst. The rats have gone so we don't need you anymore. Be off. Get out of the town before we throw you into the harbour too.'

The Pied Piper put his pipe to his mouth and played a new tune, a rollicking, playful, fun tune, and every child in the town ran and skipped and danced out into the street to join the piper, who led them from the harbour up Gold Street into Silver Street and out of the town into the forest. The tune and the sound of laughter and dancing feet gradually faded as they ran through the trees from glade to glade, and eventually it was all swallowed up amidst the old oaks and beeches and the tangled briars and nettles.

It was in vain that the townsfolk of Franchville waited for their children to return. Neither they nor the Pied Piper were ever seen again. It soon became a town populated only by old people, and an air of melancholy which could not be dispelled hung over it. And so, when the French attacked the Isle of Wight a few years later and they chose to land at Franchville, there was no one there to protect it.

THE FOUR-EYED CAT

A Story from the Fishermen of Essex
Fishermen are very superstitious folk, indeed, all seamen are superstitious. Two of the most widespread beliefs are those against whistling while at sea – it is sure to summon up a storm – and against taking a woman to sea. There are many old ballads in which a girl disguises herself as a boy in order to follow her true love over the sea, or into the navy. They can end in two very different ways: either the captain discovers her identity and keeps her for himself, or she is thrown overboard to drown once her secret comes out. This story combines both ideas.

In a seafaring town on the coast of Essex lived a gentleman who had a beautiful daughter. She was beautiful, but she was bad. This 'badness' seemed ingrained deep down in her character and she seemed to delight in doing spiteful things to upset other people. The local people thought that she was a witch and they wanted to 'swim her' – to test her in the way in which witches were tested. They'd throw her in the sea and if she swam or floated then she was a witch, so they'd push her under and drown her. If she sank then they just might … might … pull her out before she drowned and declare her innocent. That's what they would have liked to do, but they didn't dare to because of her father who was an important man.

Now this woman set her eyes on a young fisherman. The fact that he was betrothed to another local girl and they were due to marry soon didn't matter to her at all. She wanted him, so she bewitched him with her charms and soon he was following her around like Mary's little lamb. She persuaded the young man to take her with him when they next went fishing and, although he knew that it was not wise and the rest of the fleet would not allow it, he sneaked her on board his boat under the cover of darkness and they set sail.

Whether it was because that boat had a woman on board or whether it was just coincidence, I don't know, but they hadn't gone far from shore before a tremendous storm blew up, absolutely unexpectedly, and the whole fleet was lost. The families on the shore, the families of the survivors, will tell you bitterly that she deliberately whistled up the storm in order to kill the young man and to spite the rest of the people in the town.

The woman did not drown like the rest of them; she turned herself into a four-eyed cat and haunted the fishing fleet from then on. In order to appease her it became the custom for every fisherman to throw a few fish back into the sea – 'for the cat'. If anyone didn't, they would suddenly have very bad luck: things would break, they'd get lost in the mist, or they'd fish all day without catching a thing …

She only lost her power when the fishing industry went into decline and all the commercial boats ceased fishing from that port. There are still a few boatmen around who think twice before taking women to sea, and if their customers have been angling they suggest they throw something back 'for the cat'. They explain that this is just an old tradition and they have a good laugh about it, but they feel very uneasy if they don't do it.

5

DOWN ON THE FARM

THE ROARING BULL OF BAGBURY FARM

A Story from Shropshire

There once lived a very bad man at Bagbury Farm. On his deathbed he confessed that he had only ever done two good things in his whole life: the first was years ago when he was quite a young man and he had given an old waistcoat he had finished with to a poor man; and the second was that he'd once given a piece of bread and cheese to a poor beggar boy who came knocking on his door. Why he had done either of these things he couldn't explain, even to himself, but they were the sum total of the good deeds he'd done in his whole lifetime.

At last this bad man died and his body was taken and buried in the churchyard. However, his ghost would not remain quiet and returned to haunt Bagbury Farm. Whatever they did, it could not be made to leave. The ghost appeared in the shape of a huge bull, which would get into the farm buildings and roar out its challenge to the world until the walls shook and the tiles flew from the roofs. No one could bear to live nearby. At first the bull waited until nine or ten o'clock in the evening to appear, but gradually his antics began earlier and earlier until it was soon after teatime that he started his commotion.

The villagers were desperate and sent for twelve parsons to come and lay the ghost. The twelve parsons prayed and chanted, and chanted and prayed, and managed to drive the bull out of the farm buildings and up to Hyssington church, but they could not lay it. When they had it in the church all twelve parsons were praying with all their might. They were all holding candles, except for one who was blind and he had his candle stuck into the top of his boot because he didn't need it. Then the bull gave a rush to escape and all the candles went out – except for the one in the blind parson's boot. They relit the other candles from this just in time to stop the bull escaping, but the rush he made cracked the church wall from top to bottom. (That crack was allowed to stand there as a warning about the dangers of evil behaviour until the church was renovated recently.)

Well, the twelve parsons kept praying and chanting, and chanting and praying, until gradually the bull began to lose its power and to shrink. They couldn't leave off their praying for a minute to rest, though, because every time they did the bull began to regain his strength and size.

Eventually, after days of praying and chanting, and chanting and praying, the bull was about the size of a calf. They took strength from this and continued praying and chanting, and chanting and praying, until it had shrunk to the size of a kitten, and in the end it was small enough for them to trap it in a snuff box (but it still continued to stamp its feet and roar and to charge anything that came within range).

When he was safely trapped in the snuff box he stopped his roaring and began pleading with his captors. He asked them to bury the box under Bagbury Bridge, but they wouldn't because they knew that if they did every mare who crossed the bridge would lose her foal, every cow would drop its calf and every wife would become barren and never give her husband any children. Instead, they sent the box to be laid in the Red Sea for 100 years, which was a common thing to do with unwanted spirits in those days.

It is probably still there, and I suspect that the bull can do little harm there, but I also suspect that those 100 years must soon be up and I don't know what will happen then …

I do know that the local people are still, and have always been, a little bit 'shy' about going over Bagbury Bridge – they tend to creep across quickly and quietly as if they don't want to be noticed … and I don't blame them.

THE BLACK BULL OF NORROWAY

A long time ago, far over the sea in Norroway, lived a woman who had three daughters. One day her eldest daughter asked her mother to pack her up some food because she was going off to seek her fortune. The mother did so, and wished her daughter farewell, and off she went.

The girl travelled on and she travelled on until she came to the house of an old woman who was also a witch. She told the old witch-woman that she was off to seek her fortune and the old woman told her that she should come in and wait. The first morning the girl looked out of the window and she saw nothing. The second morning she looked out of the window again and still saw nothing. But the third morning, when she looked out, she saw a coach and six coming along the road. She called the old witch-woman and told her, and the old woman said, 'Well, that will be for you. Off you go,' and the girl climbed into the coach and it galloped off.

Soon the next daughter asked her mother to pack her up some food because she was going off to seek her fortune as well.

The mother did so and wished her daughter farewell, and off she went. The girl travelled on and she travelled on until she too came to the house of the old witch-woman. She told the old witch-woman that she was off to seek her fortune and the old woman told her she should come in and wait. The first morning the girl looked out of the window and she saw nothing. The second morning she looked out of the window again and still saw nothing. But the third morning, when she looked out, she saw a coach and six coming along the road. She called the old witch-woman and told her, and the old woman said, 'Well, that will be for you. Off you go,' and the girl climbed into the coach and it galloped off.

Not long after that, the youngest daughter asked her mother to pack her up some food because she, too, was going off to seek her fortune. The mother did so and wished her daughter farewell and off she went. The girl travelled on and she travelled on until she came to the house of the old witch-woman. She told the old witch-woman that she was off to seek her

fortune and the old woman told her that she should come in and wait. The first morning the girl looked out of the window and she saw nothing. The second morning she looked out of the window again and still saw nothing. But the third morning, when she looked out, she saw a great black bull walking down the road. 'Well, that will be for you,' said the old woman, 'off you go.' And, trembling with terror, the girl climbed on to the bull's back and it galloped off.

They travelled on and they travelled on until the girl grew faint with hunger and thought she must topple off the bull's broad back. Then the bull shouted back to her, 'Eat out of my right ear and drink out of my left ear and hold on tight.' So she ate out of the bull's right ear and drank out of his left ear and was wonderfully refreshed. They rode long and they rode hard until, in the distance, they saw a huge castle. 'That castle belongs to my elder brother,' said the bull. 'We will stay there for the night.'

When they reached the castle, servants came and lifted the girl down and took her into a sumptuous room to sleep, but she was too tired to appreciate the room or the furnishings! The bull was taken to a paddock to graze and to spend the night.

In the morning, after she had breakfasted, they gave her a golden apple and said that she shouldn't break it until she was in the most trouble she'd ever been in, then they lifted her on to the bull's back and away they galloped. They travelled on and they travelled on, far further than I can tell, and then they saw another castle, far grander than the first one, and far further off. 'We will sleep there tonight,' said the bull, 'for that is where my second brother lives.' Even though it was far off they soon arrived and the girl was lifted down and put to bed. It was a fine bed in a fine room, soft and luxurious, but she was too sleepy to appreciate it.

In the morning, after she had breakfasted, they gave her a golden pear and said that she shouldn't break it until she was in the most trouble she'd ever been in, then they lifted her on to the bull's back and away they galloped. They travelled far and far and further than you would believe, and then they saw another castle, even grander than the one the night before, and far further off than you can imagine. 'That is where we will spend tonight,' said the bull. 'It is the castle of my youngest brother.'

And soon they were there. Servants lifted her down and put her to sleep in a huge four-poster bed with a canopy and golden coverlets. But she was already asleep and saw none of it.

In the morning, after she had breakfasted, they gave her a golden plum and said that she shouldn't break it until she was in the most trouble she'd ever been in, then they lifted her on to the bull's back and away they galloped. On they rode and on they rode until they came to a dark and gloomy glen amongst the mountains and there they stopped. The girl climbed down and the bull said, 'Here you must wait while I go and fight the Old One. You must sit on that stone and move neither hand nor foot until I return. If you do I won't be able to find you. Wait for me, and if everything turns blue you will know that I have defeated the Old One, but if it turns red then the Old One has beaten me.'

She sat herself down and she waited and she was careful not to move neither hand nor foot. After a while, all the air around her turned blue and she was so pleased that she relaxed and crossed one foot over the other as she sat watching for the bull.

The bull returned, but however carefully and thoroughly he searched he could not find her. For a long time she sat, waiting, but at last she got up and wandered away, she didn't know where. At length she came to the foot of a mountain of glass.

She tried to climb it but she couldn't – every time she climbed up a few feet she slipped down again. She walked around the foot of the mountain until she came to a house where a smith lived. She asked the smith if he would help her get over the glass mountain and he said he would, if she agreed to work for him for seven years.

At the end of the seven years the smith made her a pair of iron shoes with spikes in them and she was able to climb the glass mountain. There she came to an old washerwoman's house. The washerwoman had a pile of clothes, all covered in blood. They had been left by a knight who had promised to marry anyone who could wash them clean. The old washerwoman had tried and tried but couldn't get the blood out, so she'd set her daughter to the task, and she tried and tried, for she would have loved to marry a knight. But however much she washed and scrubbed and lathered and rinsed she could not get the stains out either. When the girl arrived, having climbed the glass mountain, the washerwoman set her to the task and as soon as she lathered them up the water turned red and the clothes came out as white and pure as new.

When the knight returned the old washerwoman told him that it was her daughter who had washed the clothes and he agreed to marry her. The girl was heartbroken, for she had fallen in love with the knight at first glance. She decided that she was in the most trouble she'd ever been in, so she broke the apple and found that it was full of jewels. She gave them to the daughter and said that they were hers on the condition that she put off her marriage for one day and let the girl go into the knight's room alone that night. The daughter agreed, but the old woman mixed a sleeping draught and gave it to the knight who slept soundly until next morning and didn't see the visitor who sat by his bed singing:

Seven long years I served for thee,
The glassy hill I climbed for thee,
The bloody clothes I wrung for thee;
So wilt thou not waken and turn to me?

The knight did not waken, so the girl thought she was again in the most trouble she'd ever been in and broke open the pear. She found that it was full of jewels far richer than those in the apple. With them, she bargained to spend another night with the knight, but again the old woman gave him a sleeping draught and he slept the long night through while she sat by his bed singing:

Seven long years I served for thee,
The glassy hill I climbed for thee,
The bloody clothes I wrung for thee;
So wilt thou not waken and turn to me?

The next day, while they were out hunting, his companions asked the knight about the crying and moaning which they'd heard coming from his room all night. The knight said he'd heard nothing. When they assured him that they had all heard it, he said he would make a point of staying awake that night to see.

The girl, again feeling herself in the greatest trouble she had ever been in, broke open the plum and found within it the grandest jewels she'd ever seen, and with them she bought herself yet another night.

As before, the old woman brought the knight a sleeping draught but he said he couldn't drink it without some honey to sweeten it. While she was getting it he tipped the drink away but tricked the old woman into thinking he had drunk it.

Then he lay down and pretended to be asleep. Soon the girl came in and, seeing him sleeping, sat down beside him and, between sobs, sang:

Seven long years I served for thee,
The glassy hill I climbed for thee,
The bloody clothes I wrung for thee;
So wilt thou not waken and turn to me?

The knight turned and took her in his arms and told her that he was, in fact, the bull. He told her everything that had happened to him since they parted, and she told him all that had befallen her. Then he caused the old washerwoman and her daughter to be burned as witches and he married the girl and they all lived happily ever after.

THE FARMER'S THREE COWS

There was a farmer who had three cows – three fine, fat, beautiful black and white cows with big soft eyes. These fine cows gave rich, creamy milk and produced fine calves and the farmer knew that when their days were done they'd make good eating too. He made a fine living from his cows. Like all farmers with just a few animals, he gave his cows names; one was Facey, one was Diamond and the third was Beauty. He knew his animals well and was very fond of them, for this was in the time when farmers and their stock more or less shared the same living space; he and his wife lived at one end of a long farm building and the animals were at the other. It's a form of habitation which lingered on until very recently in some remote parts.

You can imagine the farmer's horror when he went into the cowshed one morning and found that, overnight, Facey had changed from a fine, fat, beautiful animal into a bag of skin and bones. She looked like an old kite with her skin hanging loose and her eyes dull and sad. Also puzzling was the fact that in the fireplace was a pile of wood ash. The farmer and his wife could think of no explanation, for they hadn't lit a fire there.

The next morning it happened to be the wife who went into the cowshed first and she found Diamond looking just as bad as Facey. And the fireplace was piled up three feet high with wood ash. What was happening?

The farmer decided that he would keep watch that night to see what was happening, so he hid himself in a cupboard in the kitchen and left the door between the house and the cowshed open. Time passed very slowly and the breathing of the animals almost lulled him to sleep. He had great trouble in keeping himself awake. In fact he was about to give up and tell himself he was wasting his time when, suddenly, the door opened and in ran what seemed like a thousand pixies, all laughing and screeching. They grabbed Beauty's halter and dragged her into the middle of the room where they threw her down on to the floor and killed her. Then the knives flew and, as quick as lightning, Beauty was skinned and every scrap of meat scraped from her bones.

More pixies poured in through the door carrying firewood and soon there was a blaze in the hearth and meat was roasting and baking and boiling and frying. The chief of the pixies called out, 'Be careful, make sure not a bone gets broken!'

When they had eaten every scrap of food the pixies played games with the bones, tossing them to each other and playing five-stones and dice. One little bone flew through the air and landed just outside the cupboard where the farmer was hiding.

He was frightened that the pixies might find him if they came to retrieve it and he hated to think what punishment they would mete out to him if they did, so he reached out a hand and took in the bone.

The farmer continued hiding in the cupboard and the pixies continued their revels until the first faint glimmer of dawn appeared at the window. 'Morning is coming, gather up the bones!' called the chief pixie, and they rushed around and picked up every one. Then they assembled them into the skeleton of a cow, all in their proper places, and they draped the skin of Beauty over it. Then the chief pixie tapped it with his wand and the cow gave a great sigh, staggered to her feet and lowed in a melancholy tone. The pixies led her back to her stall, but she limped on one hind foot because there was one tiny bone missing.

'The cock crew
Away they flew'

... and the farmer crept trembling to bed.

The Dun Cow of Durham

This story brings together a major figure from British ecclesiastical history and an animal very common in English folklore. St Cuthbert, one of the earliest British saints, is still revered in the North of England, and the dun cow crops up all over the country. I have no idea how many Dun Cow pubs there are, but it must be a lot, and many stories mention a dun cow as a very minor 'character'. No one seems to know quite what a 'dun cow' was – it's usually just defined as 'a brown-coloured cow' but they seem to have been a specific type of cow, perhaps not a breed as we would now define it but something distinct, and they were, apparently, famous for their milk and for their quiet character – rather like a Jersey or Guernsey.

St Cuthbert lived in Northumbria (northern England/ southern Scotland) in the seventh century CE, a time when Christianity in Britain was deciding whether to follow the rules of the old Celtic Church or to go with Rome. Cuthbert followed Rome and was made Prior of Lindisfarne, but he continued to do missionary work throughout Britain. The incident with the dun cow happened after his death.

Cuthbert died in 687 and was buried at Lindisfarne, but at that time all the monasteries along the north-east coast were being raided by Vikings so it was decided to move his coffin to a safer place inland. A group of monks, with a long procession of followers, set out to do this. They were not sure where they were heading but were aiming for Chester-le-Street as a first stop. When they reached the hill of Warden Law, near Sunderland, the bier carrying the coffin stopped and could not be made to move a fraction of an inch in any direction. For three days they waited and prayed, hoping for a miracle, or directions from above. At last St Cuthbert appeared to one of the monks, called Eadmer, and told him that the coffin should be taken to a place called Dun Holm.

After that the bier moved with no trouble, but no one knew where Dun Holm was. They continued their way along the road asking for Dun Holm but with no luck. Later that day, when they were at a place called Mount Joy, a milkmaid approached the procession. She said that she had lost her dun cow and asked whether anyone had seen it. The only clue she had as to where it might be was that she had last seen it at Dun Holm. The monks suggested that she return there to see

if it had made its way back home and they followed after her. They found themselves on a rise or island in a tight meander on the River Wear. There they buried St Cuthbert and built the first church on the site, which now houses the magnificent Durham Cathedral.

Durham is probably my favourite British cathedral and a city I like a lot, too. If you visit and explore it you will see a panel on the north facade of the cathedral depicting the milkmaid and her cow and, not far from the cathedral, down Dun Cow Lane, you will find the Dun Cow pub.

The name Durham comes from Old English meaning an island with a hill. Whether or not the milkmaid was reunited with her cow is not recorded.

FOUR ANIMALS SEEK THEIR FORTUNE

One day a bull, a tup, a cock and a gander, having grown tired of life in the farmyard, set out to seek their fortune. (They'd probably heard the farmer's wife reading her children stories of Jack and other young men – and women! – who did similar things.) They walked off down the road and, as night began to fall, they came to a house. They knocked on the door and asked for a bed for the night. The people in the house said they didn't have any spare beds – they were only poor people – but the four animals could sleep in the kitchen where it would be warmer than outside in the barn. The four friends thanked them.

The bull said he'd lie on the floor and the tup said he'd curl up by his side. The cock was going to lie on the rannel-baulk – the beam over the fireplace where the pots were suspended – because there it would be nice and warm, and the gander said he'd sit by the back door to guard the place.

The animals lay down in their chosen places and went off to sleep, but at midnight they were woken by scuffles outside and they heard whispering voices. It was two men planning to rob the house. The men decided which of them would climb in and which would keep watch outside.

After a few minutes a window opened and one of the men clambered through. No sooner had his feet touched the ground than the bull butted him and the tup did likewise. The cock crowed, 'Bring him here and I'll peck out his eyes!' The man beat a hasty retreat out through the door, and as he did so the gander pecked him on his nose and beat him with his wings. When he stumbled out into the yard the other man looked at him in amazement. 'What have you been doing?' he asked.

'Me? Doing?' stuttered the man. 'Why I did nothing, but don't go in there. The Devil himself is in there and he knocked me about and then his imps took over and knocked me about a bit more. A thin, shivering creature said, "bring him here and I'll put out his eyes", and as I was escaping through the door a blacksmith got me with a pair of tongs and flapped me round the ears with his leather apron!'

Without more ado the two men beat a hasty retreat and the four travellers settled down to a good sleep.

This story from Yorkshire is obviously a version of the Grimms' 'The Town Musicians of Bremen'.

6

BREAD AND CIRCUSES

Stories of Showmen and Their Animals

THE FLYING DONKEYS OF DERBY

Some of you, indeed many of you, may well have visited the storytelling events in Derby which go under the title of 'The Flying Donkeys'. They've been running for more than twenty years. You may have wondered what the title means and how it came about. Here is the true story.

Back in the 1730s the latest craze from the Continent reached Derby. It was called 'flying', although in reality there was no actual flight involved – unless something went very wrong, that is!

'Flying' was brought to Derby by a travelling French showman, M. Gillinoe. What he actually did was to stretch a rope from the top of the tower of the church of All Saints (now Derby Cathedral) to the nearby, much lower, tower of the chapel of St Mary's. Then, clad in a metal breastplate, he slid down the rope blowing a trumpet and firing a pistol! The 'flight' took about eight seconds. Every day he performed this stunt twice to ever-increasing crowds. The craze caught on and soon daredevils all over the town were sliding down ropes strung from houses, trees and walls. Animals were made to take part and races were held. I would guess that there were many injuries, but possibly no fatalities – at least no record of them has come down to us.

When M. Gillinoe moved on to take his amusement to other places his mantle as 'chief flyer' was taken on by a local lad called Cadman. Cadman used wood rather than a metal breast-plate and sometimes his 'flights' were so fast that he finished in a cloud of smoke caused by friction! He was a showman and flew on his back, his front, sitting up, laying down, and even standing on one leg!

Cadman's superiority was overturned in 1734 when a man arrived with a donkey. He said he'd make the donkey fly! He started by sliding down the rope himself with a wheelbarrow in which intrepid (foolhardy?) locals could hitch a ride. One passenger was the mayor!

Then came the time for the donkey. It had been taken to the top of the tower the day before from whence it could be heard braying – perhaps it could foresee what was going to happen! Somehow it was manoeuvred on to the rope with heavy weights attached to its feet to keep it stable. It began to slide, but when it was almost to the ground the rope broke and it toppled on to the crowd. No one was killed but quite a few were injured and the showman and his donkey beat a hasty retreat and were never seen in Derby again.

That was the end of the 'flying' craze and of real 'flying donkeys', but the image lingered on.

The present Derby Cathedral building dates from 1725, so it was new when the above happened, although the tower is older, dating back to the early 1500s. It is 212 feet high and houses the oldest ring of ten bells in the country. The tenor bell is even older than the tower. A carillon uses the bells to play tunes – one of which is the 'Derby Ram', although it is the slow march of the Sherwood Forester Regiment, not the famous folk song.

It seems that in the eighteenth and nineteenth centuries Britain was full of foreign showmen and their animals – not just donkeys, but bears and monkeys and even elephants and tigers! Being an animal showman seems to have been a precarious occupation, though, and they and their animals definitely weren't always treated well.

At Wirksworth, in Derbyshire, there was an Italian showman who had a monkey. He used to send this monkey down into the lead mines carrying food and messages for the miners, but one day it didn't come back. There is a plaque commemorating this on the High Peak Trail near the National Stone Centre. I wonder if there is a ghostly monkey still living in the caves under Wirksworth …

A little further north a pair of 'Royal Bengal Tigers' escaped from a menagerie in Sheffield in 1789. They made their way across the countryside into Derbyshire where they killed a child. The impressively named Sir Sitwell Sitwell, of Renshaw Hall, leapt at the opportunity to hunt and kill the tigers, for he was a great sportsman and kept racehorses and hounds as well as indulging in fishing and shooting. It made a nice change to have tigers to shoot at instead of the usual pheasants and hares.

WHO KILLED THE BEARS?

A Story from the Forest of Dean

In April 1889 four Frenchmen with two dancing bears arrived in the Forest of Dean and performed at Cinderford. The bears were Russian black bears and they were muzzled and chained, but they delighted their audiences by 'dancing' through the streets to the music played by their keepers. The bears were very popular and it was a profitable day for the Frenchmen.

However, after they'd left town word went around that the bears were fed on human flesh and that a local child had been killed and a woman mauled. When this rumour reached the local pubs a mob of nearly 200 drunken, angry foresters gathered and went out looking for the Frenchmen. When they were caught they were badly beaten with sticks and stones. Two of them hid in the woods, while the other two were given shelter by local householders in Ruardean. One of the bears was killed then and there and the other was later shot near Ross-on-Wye.

Later that evening when the police investigated, it became obvious that neither the bears nor their keepers had committed any crime whatsoever, so fourteen men were arrested and charged with attacking the Frenchmen and killing the bears. They were fined a total of £85, which was a huge amount for those times. Although all the culprits were from Cinderford, the story somehow attached itself to Ruardean and the inhabitants of that town were teased about it mercilessly. In fact, even 150 years later, it is still very unwise to ask in the town, 'Who killed the bears?'

The Congleton Bear

One of the first things I did in preparation for this book was to post a question on Facebook asking my followers if they knew of any animals associated with their town or county. The most popular ones were 'The Derby Ram' and 'The Hartlepool Monkey'. There were lots of others, but they were mainly the mascots of the local football team and there was very little actual *story* to them. 'The Congleton Bear' was a story which many people knew – it's another one about travelling showmen and what they get up to.

Back in the 1620s one of the most popular sights at the Wakes, in the Cheshire town of Congleton, was the dancing bear. (Other popular events, besides freak shows and wrestling, were bear-baiting, cockfighting and dogfighting!) In this particular year though, Congleton had no dancing bear. One version of the story says that the bear had become too old to dance, another says that it had died, but whatever the reason Congleton needed a new bear. And they couldn't afford it.

Then one of the town councillors remembered that they had a sum of money put aside to buy a new Bible for the parish church. He suggested that they should borrow that money and pay it back from the profits generated by their new bear, which they did.

People like to gossip though, and if they can 'dig the dirt', they will. The story which got around, and which has survived to the present day, is that the people of Congleton sold the church Bible to buy a new bear! That story stuck and Congleton is still called 'Bear Town' and has a bear as its emblem. They are proud of their bear, just as the inhabitants of Hartlepool are proud of hanging their monkey ...

THE HARTLEPOOL MONKEY

This is another of the stories which everyone knows and expects to find in this book. It is unusual in that what started as a derogatory joke about the inhabitants of Hartlepool has been transformed into something they are now proud of! The local Rugby Union team, Hartlepool Rovers, are known as the 'Monkeyhangers' and the football team, Hartlepool United, have a monkey mascot called 'H'Angus'. In 2002 Stuart Drummond campaigned for the office of Mayor of

Hartlepool dressed in the costume of H'Angus the monkey and won! His election slogan was 'free bananas for school-children', a promise he was unable to keep, but he has been re-elected twice since.

Why a monkey in Hartlepool? It goes back to the times of the Napoleonic Wars. Very few Hartlepudlians would have ever seen a Frenchman and had no idea what one looked like, but they, like everyone else along the coast, were terrified of a French invasion and of French spies. The coast around North Yorkshire and Cleveland is notoriously dangerous, a graveyard for ships that get caught on the 'lee shore' – a gale which blows your ship on to the coast. (You may remember that it was down that same coast at Whitby that Dracula came ashore in the shape of a huge, black dog when the ship *Demeter* was caught in just such a storm.)

One December day, a French ship called the *Chasse Maree* was seen struggling just offshore near the Hartlepool headland. A storm was raging and it was hard to see the ship through the rain and waves. It must have been equally hard for the crew of the ship to see where they were, and after a while the ship floundered. Next morning a lot of wreckage and some bodies were washed ashore, but only one survivor – a little man just a foot or two high dressed in a military uniform. Perhaps all Frenchmen were like this? He definitely wasn't an Englishman, for he had a tail and Englishmen don't have tails! Also, he didn't appear to speak English.

The monkey was captured and a trial was held on the beach, where he was condemned as being a French spy. The punishment for spies was the gallows, so the monkey was hanged from the mast of a fishing boat and the fishermen were then able to return to the more profitable business of collecting useful items from the wreckage.

Alan Wilkinson of the well-known local folk group, 'The Teesside Fettlers', wrote a very popular song about the incident which I've heard sung no end of times. The chorus goes:

Singing old folks, young folks, everyone and each
Have come to see the Frenchie who's landed on the beach.
He's got long arms and a great long tail and he's covered down in hair.
We think that he's a spy, so we'll hang him in the square!

THE MAN, THE BOY AND THE DONKEY

One day a man and his young son were on their way to market. They had with them the family donkey which was going to carry their purchases home. As they were going along the way they met a traveller going in the opposite direction and, as he passed, he said, 'You silly man, why walk when you've got a donkey? A donkey is for riding.' The man saw the sense of this, so he lifted up his son and put him on the donkey's back.

They went on a bit further and met a group of people standing by the road side. As they passed the father heard them say, 'Look at that lazy, young good-for-nothing. He lets his poor old father walk while he rides.' The man lifted down his son and climbed up on to the donkey himself.

Soon they passed two women, also going to market. 'Shame on you,' they said. 'To let your poor little boy trudge along while a big, strong man like you rides!' He didn't know what to do, so he lifted up his son in front of him and they both rode on.

Soon though, they were shouted at by some more travellers who said it wasn't fair for that poor little donkey to have to carry both of them. The man and his son both climbed down and the man tried to think what to do. Then he went and cut a long pole. They tied the donkey's feet together and slung it under the pole and they set off down the road carrying the donkey between them. Everyone they met burst into gales of laughter when they saw this.

At last, just as they were approaching the market, the donkey, frightened by all the noise and feeling helpless, got a foot loose and lashed out. This caused the boy to drop the pole and the donkey plunged over the wall, off the bridge and into the river where it was drowned.

And the moral of this tale is: if you try to please everyone you'll please no one.

This is one of the stories from Aesop's Fables, *but it has almost removed itself from that category and become a folk tale in its own right. As I said in the introduction, I considered having a little set of* Aesop's Fables *as they've been in print in English since they were published by Caxton in 1484 – more than half a millennium ago. They've influenced and educated generations of Britons but they are still tagged as* 'Aesop's Fables' *and are thought of as Greek rather than British, so in the end I decided not to, apart from the odd sneaky one which hid away.*

JACK AND THE DEAD DONKEY

Showmen with donkeys can still make a living – think of all those donkey rides on beaches and in parks – and the donkey doesn't even have to be alive! Here's a modern shaggy dog story (can you have a shaggy donkey story?).

Jack was a city boy, but when he grew up he moved to the country. He bought himself a nice house with a piece of land and thought he'd have some animals to go on it. The first animal he got was an old donkey which he bought from a farmer for £100. The farmer said he'd deliver the donkey the next day. (As I said, Jack was a city boy, I'm sure he could have got an old donkey for a lot less – even for nothing!)

The next day, the farmer drove up and said, 'Sorry, old son, but I have some bad news for you. The donkey died.'

Jack replied, 'Well, just give me my money back, then.'

'I can't do that, I've spent it already,' the farmer said.

'OK, then, just give me the donkey.'

'What do you want a dead donkey for?' asked the farmer, puzzled.

Jack said, 'I'm going to raffle him off.'

'You can't raffle off a dead donkey!' said the farmer.

'Sure I can. Just watch me. I just won't tell anybody he is dead.'

A month later, the farmer met Jack in the village and asked, 'What happened with that dead donkey?'

Jack said, 'I raffled him off like I said I would. I sold 500 tickets at £2 each and made a profit of £898.'

The farmer asked, 'Didn't anyone complain?'

Jack replied, 'Only the chap who won, so I gave him his £2 back. That's why the profit wasn't a round £900.'

Jack grew up to become the chairman of a multinational company.

This is a modern folk tale that is probably very recent, but it fulfils all the criteria to be 'traditional' – it has its roots in far older stories, it's anonymous and it has changed through repeated transmission from one teller to another. Most traditional tales have been told orally, but many of these modern ones are transmitted via the internet and email. That has the effect of shrinking time and what took hundreds of years to happen to a story in 'the old days' now happens within weeks.

THE PARROT

An Old Story from Yorkshire

In a quaint little town in Yorkshire there once lived a grocer who had a beautiful, bright green parrot called Polly. Polly lived in a cage by his shop door and greeted everyone who came into the shop. Sometimes it was a very nice greeting – 'Hello. Good day.' – but at other times it was rather rude – 'Look out. Here comes the old bat.' Sometimes the parrot was even ruder and used language the owner swore she must have picked up before she came to live with him because she would never have heard those words in his shop! No one minded too much, though, because she was just a parrot and she didn't really know what she was saying … or did she …?

In fact Polly was a very shrewd, sensible bird, and saw everything that happened in the shop. Unfortunately she couldn't help shouting out all the little things she noticed, often without warning, and sometimes at the most awkward moment.

One day Polly noticed her master 'stretching' the brown sugar by mixing a little sand into the sack. A bit later on, in came a woman and asked for some brown sugar. 'Sand in the sugar! Sand in the sugar!' squawked the parrot, and the customer pocketed her money and rushed out of the shop.

The angry grocer rushed to the cage and shook it. 'You abominable bird!' he shouted. 'If you tell tales again I'll wring your neck!' And again he shook the cage till the poor creature was all ruffled up and a cloud of feathers was flying around the shop.

Next day the parrot saw its master mixing brick dust into the cocoa powder. Just afterwards in came a customer asking for cocoa. 'Brick dust in the cocoa! Brick dust in the cocoa!' cried Polly, loudly and repeatedly until the astonished customer believed it, and went away without his cocoa. There followed another shaking of the cage and a warning that any more tale-telling would certainly be punished with death!

The frightened parrot promised never to speak again.

Presently, however, it observed its master making 'shop butter' from lard coloured with a little turmeric. Then in came a lady and asked for butter.

'Nice fresh butter, ma'am, fresh from the dairy,' said the shopkeeper.

'Lard in the butter! Lard in the butter!' screamed the parrot, and the woman turned and left the shop.

'You worthless bird!' yelled the shopkeeper and rushed to the cage. He opened the door, pulled out the parrot, wrung its neck and threw it into the ash pit.

But Polly was not quite dead, and after lying quiet for a few minutes she lifted up her head and saw a dead cat in the pit with her. 'Hello!' called the parrot. 'What's the matter with you, Tom?'

There was no answer for the cat really was dead.

'Oh dear, poor Tom,' sighed the parrot. 'He too must have loved the truth and been punished for speaking it.'

Polly sat up and tried her wings. They were undamaged. She stretched her legs and looked all round. She seemed unharmed, but she was hurt in her soul. Polly lamented, 'Oh, great is the truth in my own country, but in this dingy, dark England it is held for nothing. Lies are all that count here – lies and profit.'

Then Polly spread her wings and flew away. Whether she ever reached her own land, where truth was held in such high regard, I don't know. More likely she flew twice round the world in search of it, and could not find it, for in today's world I doubt that such a place exists.

The Frog at the Well

This is one of the best-known folk tale motifs in a version from the North of England – it was a Scottish version of this story which inspired the Brothers Grimm to start their collection!

One morning a young woman took her jug and went down to the well to fetch some water, but when she got there she found the well had gone dry. So she sat on the edge of the well and started to cry. Now, any of you modern, capable, educated women reading this wouldn't behave in that way, would you? You'd know how to get the well unblocked or would call the plumber or phone for a delivery of bottled water from a supermarket, or something … but none of those options were open to her, so she just sat on the edge of the well, and cried.

As she was sitting there crying, a frog came plopping along the path towards her and when it got there it said, 'Hello, why are you crying?'

'Because the well's gone dry and there's no water.'

'Well, if you marry me then you can have all the water you want,' said the frog.

The young woman didn't fancy marrying a frog – she didn't know anyone who had married a frog. None of her friends had married frogs, but she couldn't really think of any good reason not to, so she said, 'Alright', and when she looked the well was full of water. Without giving the frog another thought she filled her jug and went home.

That night, when she and her mother were getting ready for bed, there was a sudden commotion outside the door and someone started singing:

'Open the door, my hinny, my heart
Open the door, my deary,
Remember the promise that you and I made
Down in the meadow so early.'

'Who's that singing outside the door?' asked the mother.

'Oh, it must be that old frog I met down by the well this morning.'

'Well, let him in, it's cold out there.'

So the girl let him in and he sat down by the fire and got warm and then he sang:

'Give me my supper, my hinny, my heart
Give me my supper, my deary,
Remember the promise that you and I made
Down in the meadow so early.'

And the mother sent the daughter into the kitchen to bring the frog some supper. She wasn't quite sure what a frog would want for supper so she piled up a tray with all kinds of things and brought it back, and the frog ate the lot. Then it licked its lips and burped and sang:

'Put me to bed, my hinny, my heart
Put me to bed, my deary,
Remember the promise that you and I made
Down in the meadow so early.'

So the girl went into the bedroom and did all the things you do to a visitor's bed – she puffed up the pillows and tucked in the sheets and smoothed out the blankets and the frog jumped into bed, and then he looked at her and sang:

'Jump into bed, my hinny, my heart
Jump into bed, my deary,
Remember the promise that you and I made
Down in the meadow so early.'

Now she didn't much fancy getting into bed with a frog, but her mother had made her do everything else so she didn't think it was worth arguing. So she got into bed and lay down on one side while the frog was the other side and she made sure there was a big gap down the middle of the bed between them. But the frog looked at her and sang:

'Give me a kiss, my hinny, my heart
Give me a kiss, my deary,
Remember the promise that you and I made
Down in the meadow so early.'

So she screwed up her eyes and she screwed up her lips and she screwed up her courage and she screwed up everything else which she could think of to possibly screw up, and she leaned over and gave the frog a quick little peck on the lips.

And when she opened her eyes ... I'm sure you have guessed, instead of a frog there was the most handsome young man she'd seen in her whole life, and he said, 'Thank you, you've saved me from a wicked enchantment,' – and what happened next I will leave to your imagination!

LOVE FROGS

A modern variant of the above.

A beautiful young woman was feeling lonely so went to her local pet shop in search of an exotic pet. As she looked about the shop she noticed a tank full of frogs. A sign said:

LOVE FROG'S. SUCCESS GUARANTEED. COME'S WITH INSTRUCTION'S

(As is the way with these things the sign was complete with unnecessary apostrophes!)

The woman looked around to see if anybody was watching and then went up and whispered softly to the young man behind the counter, 'I'll take one.'

The man put the frog into a little plastic tank and said, 'Make sure you follow the instructions carefully.' The woman nodded and took the frog home.

As soon as she had closed the door to her flat she read the instructions thoroughly, and carefully did as they said:

1. Take a shower.
2. Splash on some nice-smelling perfume.
3. Place the frog in the bed and climb in beside it.

She got into bed with the frog but nothing happened.

She re-read the instructions.

Still nothing happened.

Then she noticed that, at the bottom of the page, there was a note which said, 'If you have any problems or questions please call the pet shop.' So she called the pet shop.

The man said, 'That's odd, I had another complaint earlier today, too. I'll come over straight away.'

Within five minutes, her doorbell rang. The woman welcomed him in and said, 'See, I've done everything according to the instructions but the frog just sits there.'

The man, looking very concerned, picked up the frog, stared directly into its eyes and said sternly, 'Listen to me! I'm only going to show you how to do this one more time …'

7

WE THREE KINGS

HOW THE HERRING BECAME THE KING OF THE SEA

A Manx Tale

One day the fish decided that they needed someone to rule over them – a king. They didn't have a deemster – a magistrate or judge – like the people on the Isle of Man, so it seemed a good idea. They called a meeting somewhere in the deeps off the Shoulder, near the Calf of Man, and they all arrived looking their best, for you have to look your best if you want to be voted king!

All the fish were there: Captain Jiarg, the red gurnet, in his fine crimson coat; Grey Horse, the big, cruel shark; Bollan, the wrass, in his brightest colours; Dirty Peggy, the cuttlefish, putting on her nicest face; Athag, the haddock, trying to rub

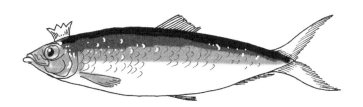

out the black spots the Devil burned on him when he took hold of him with his finger and thumb; and all the rest of the fish from the smallest to the largest. Each one thought he had a good chance and hoped he might be chosen.

The fish had a strong notion to make Brac Gorm, the mackerel, king. He was the pre-meeting favourite. He knew that, so he put beautiful stripes on himself, pink and green and gold and all the colours of the sea and sky, and then he added sparkling diamonds. When he arrived in all this finery he looked so grand that they didn't recognise him and they ignored him.

In the end Skeddan, the herring, 'the Lil Silver Fella', was made the King of the Sea and everyone agreed that it was a good choice.

When it was all over, up rushed the fluke, too late to give his vote, and they all called out, 'You've missed the tide, my beauty!' He had been so busy titivating himself up, touching himself up with red patches, that he forgot the time. When he found that the herring had been chosen he twisted up his mouth and sneered, 'And what am I going to be then?' Scarrag the skate gave him such a slap with his tail that it knocked the fluke's mouth even more to one side and it's been crooked like that ever since.

The herring is still the King of the Sea and that may be why he is so honoured amongst men, particularly on the Isle of Man. When the deemsters there take their oath they say, 'I will execute justice as indifferently as the herring's backbone doth lie in the midst of the fish'. And the Manx people will not burn a herring's bones in the fire in case the herring should feel it. Those that know, say that the best herring in the world are caught in that place off the Shoulder, where the fish held their big meeting.

The names of the fish above are the Manx names. The same story, with local names, is found in the Scottish islands and is probably common amongst fishermen all around the coast, as the song below, from East Anglia, includes the same ideas.

Windy Old Weather

One night we were fishing off Happisburgh* Light,
Fishing and trawling, all through the night

Chorus: In this windy old weather, stormy old weather,
When the wind blows we'll all pull together.

Up jumped the herring, the King of the Sea,
He sang out 'Old Skipper, O you can't catch me!'

Up jumped the mackerel with spots on his back,
He sang out, 'Old Skipper, come square your main tack!'

Up jumped the crab with his great long claws,
He sang out, 'Old Skipper, you'll run her ashore!'

Up jumped the rooker, his back hard and tough,
He sang out, 'Old Skipper, you will burn the duff!'

Up jumped the sprat, the smallest of all,
He sang out, 'Old Skipper, you will lose your trawl!'

Up jumped the whiting with silvery eyes
Said, 'You haven't got long on the sea for to ride!'

Up spoke the skipper, 'The saying is right,
We'll haul up our trawl and we'll go home tonight!'

This is a song which was very popular amongst East Anglian fishermen. It was famously sung by Harry Cox, who was the source of many great songs.

*Happisburgh is pronounced 'Haiseborough'.

The King of the Fishes

A few of the stories in this book can be found in the two collections by Joseph Jacobs: English Fairy Tales *and* More English Fairy Tales. *Jacobs (1854–1916) was, in a way, the British equivalent of the Brothers Grimm. This tale is not in either of those collections, but it is in another of his books called* Europa's Fairy Book, *in which he attempted to 'complete' folk tales by correlating different versions from all over Europe. I have used just the beginning of the story, which can stand on its own. Jacobs goes on to tell, at great length, of the exploits of George and Albert. (Unusual names for a fairy tale, but very fashionable at the time he was writing.)*

Once upon a time there was a fisherman who was very poor. He felt poorer still because he and his wife had no children. They wanted children and they had tried to have them, but children never arrived. One day when he was fishing he caught the finest fish he had ever seen. It was large enough to provide several meals for him and his wife, but it also looked grand; its scales were golden and its eyes were as bright as diamonds. He was just going to take it out of his net and take it home when it spoke. 'I am the King of the Fishes,' it said. 'If you throw me back into the water you will never want for a catch.' The fisherman was so surprised that he let the fish slip back into the water. Once it was safe it flapped its big tail and dived under the waves.

When the fisherman got home he told his wife all about it, and she said, 'Oh, you silly man, I'd love to eat a fish like that.'

The next day the fisherman went fishing again in the same place and, sure enough, he caught the same fish again, and it said, 'I am the King of the Fishes, if you let me go you shall always find your nets full.' So the fisherman let him go again. When he got back home he told his wife what he had done and she began to cry and wail and said, 'I told you I wanted such a fish, but you let him go. You don't love me!'

The fisherman did love his wife very much indeed, and he felt ashamed of himself, so he promised that if he caught the King of the Fishes again he would bring him home to his wife for her to cook.

The next day the fisherman went to the same place and caught the same fish for the third time. But when the fish begged the fisherman to let him go he told the King of the Fishes what his wife had said and what he had promised her. 'Well,' said the King of the Fishes, 'if you must kill me then kill me you must, but as you've let me go twice I will do this for you. When your wife cuts me up she must throw some of my bones under the mare, and some of my bones under the bitch, and the rest of my bones she must bury beneath the rose tree in the garden and then you will see what you will see.'

So the fisherman took the King of the Fishes home to his wife and he told her what the fish had said. That evening, when she cut up the fish for cooking, she threw some of the bones under the mare, and some under the bitch, and the rest she buried under the rose tree in the garden.

A few months later, the fisherman's wife found that she was, at last, pregnant, and when the time came she gave birth to two fine twin boys. Just under the hair on their foreheads each had a star. They named them George and Albert, for those were the names which were popular for boys at that time. At the same time the mare brought into the world two fine colts, and the bitch two puppies and they all had identical stars on their foreheads!

Under the very ordinary rambling rose tree grew up two fine rose bushes, each of which bore, every year, only a single rose, but what a splendid rose it was! It lasted all through the summer and long into the winter and, most curious of all, when George fell ill one of the roses began to wilt, and if Albert wasn't well the other rose faded.

The fisherman and his wife lived happily together and George and Albert grew up to be fine young men. They went on to have many adventures and both married princesses and ruled their own lands. And all thanks to the King of the Fishes.

I don't know what happened to the fisherman and his wife. I assume they lived out their days very happily with their long awaited family and plenty of fish in their nets.

If this story has a moral or a lesson to teach then I'm not quite sure what it is. The fisherman had pity on the fish twice but then went back on his word when his wife tried a bit of moral blackmail. The fish did keep his word and rewarded the fisherman with far more than he deserved. Like most folk tales, this one does not stand analysis so just enjoy it as a bit of fun.

THE KING OF THE BIRDS

The wren, the wren, the king of birds
His brood is big, but he is small.

One day the birds held a meeting. They all
got together to decide things and to discuss
important matters. There they were, all
sitting around and chirruping to each
other – you know how these meetings
go, everyone talking to everyone else
about things which don't matter, not
finishing one conversation before they start
on another with someone else. Most of it was
just idle chatter, but every now and again one
would give a loud squawk and say something
worth saying.

One of the birds said that he'd been watching Man and every group of men seemed to
have a king. Perhaps the birds should have a
king too, he said. It would make it easier to
make decisions and meetings would be much
shorter. The other birds all thought this
sounded a good idea, but how were they going
to decide which bird should be king?

Everyone chipped in with their different
ideas:

The biggest bird.
The strongest bird.
The bird who could fly furthest.
The bird who could fly fastest.

The bird who could stay in the air for the longest.
The bird who could sing loudest.
The bird with the most beautiful song.
The bird with the prettiest feathers.
The bird with the longest beak.
The bird with the longest tail.

The list was endless ...

I don't know how they came to a conclusion, but the suggestion they decided on was the bird who could fly highest.

One of the birds who was loudest in its support for this idea was, surprisingly, the wren – the little, tiny wren who flitters around in the shadows down by the ground and is rarely seen.

So, at the appointed time all the birds met together again and competed with each other to see which could fly highest. Some could not fly very high at all, just a little above the tree tops; others soared up into the clouds until they could hardly be seen; but the one who beat them all was the eagle. Up and up and up he went until he was higher than any of the other birds had been. The eagle was king.

But what was that? Just as eagle could go no higher and started to come down again a tiny spot launched itself from the feathers on eagle's back and fluttered a few more feet into the air. It was the wren. He had hitched a ride on eagle's back and now he had flown higher than any other bird, including eagle. The wren had won. The wren was king.

Or was he?

Did it count?

Was it cheating?

Did they want their king to be chosen in that way?

The birds turned to the wise owl and asked him what he thought. The owl turned his head to the east, and then he turned it to the west; he turned it north, he turned it south and then he turned it right round. Then the owl gave his decision. The wren had played a clever trick, but a clever trickster didn't deserve to be the king. The eagle was the king. He had won the right and won it fairly.

And so it is. The eagle is the King of the Birds and the wren still flitters around in the undergrowth under the hedge, but every now and again he finds a nice pole to sit on and sings out to everyone, in a voice that seems far too loud for such a tiny bird, about how he flew higher than the eagle and could, or perhaps should, have been the King of the Birds.

8

HERE COMES
THE CAVALRY

THE LION AND THE UNICORN

The lion and the unicorn
Were fighting for the crown,
The lion beat the unicorn
All around the town.

In this old nursery rhyme the lion is, of course, England and the unicorn is Scotland. The fight still goes on and probably always will! The unicorn has been a part of the royal seal of Scotland since at least the 1300s when Robert III turned to it as a symbol of purity and strength when he was trying to rebuild the nation.

When James VI of Scotland became James I of England he combined the Scottish unicorn with the English lion, which was perhaps not a wise choice as a Babylonian myth going back to 3,500 BCE points out that the lion and the unicorn are implacable enemies!

The unicorn is not really a horse, though. Or is it? It seems to inhabit a no-man's-land between a horse, a goat and a fairy creature. Although everyone knows about unicorns, and they occur in all kinds of literature – especially children's literature – there is very little British folklore about them.

Strangely, the same is true about horses generally. We are a nation who love horses and equestrianism but we don't seem to go in for folk tales about them. We have acquired a few horses from other mythologies but they haven't been adopted as British. Interestingly, most of these are white horses, which have always been 'special'.

From Greek mythology we have taken Pegasus and the Norse have loaned us Odin's horse, Sleipnir, with its eight legs! In Celtic mythology, Rhiannon rides a 'pale white horse', as does St George. (And the tradition continues down through Roy Rogers to Clint Eastwood and many other Western heroes!) Two of the Four Horsemen of the Apocalypse ride white or pale horses – Pestilence on the white and Death on the pale one.

As the King James Bible puts it in Revelation 6:8:

And I looked, and behold a pale horse: and his name that sat on him was Death, and Hell followed with him. And power was

given unto them over the fourth part of the earth, to kill with
sword, and with hunger, and with death, and with the beasts of
the earth.

It seems very likely that the Bronze Age inhabitants of the
South of England worshipped horses or, at least, held them in
high esteem. They may have been 'badges', for they appear on
early coins and, of course, were carved, hugely, on chalk hill-
sides. Many of those which survive are comparatively recent
but the famous one at Uffington dates back to the Bronze Age,
if not earlier.

The white horse as a territorial badge survives to the present
in the coat of arms of Kent, one of the oldest kingdoms.
Fittingly the next story comes from that county.

GREY DOLPHIN'S REVENGE

Back in the fourteenth century there lived a knight called Sir
Roger de Shurland. Sir Roger owned land on the north coast
of Kent which included the Isle of Sheppey. He had a rich hall
and farmed a large area of land. On the whole he was a good
man and a good farmer who treated his people well – or as well
as any knight treated his serfs in those days. The one drawback
to Sir Roger was that he had a terrible temper. He would be
quiet and thoughtful, kind and caring, but then something
would annoy him and without the slightest warning he would
lash out.

As he grew older he learned to control his temper or, at
least, to take himself off to where it would do no harm. This
he did by riding. When he felt things getting on top of him,
Sir Roger would mount his horse, Grey Dolphin, and ride full

pelt through the fields or over the downs or along the beach until he had regained control of himself. They got by in this fashion for many years.

Then, one Good Friday, a monk came to Sir Roger and begged him to allow his workers to have a day off so that they could go to church and pray. But Sir Roger wanted his men to finish ploughing some fields before the weather broke. The monk would not take 'no' for an answer and continued to argue his case until Sir Roger lost his temper. With no warning he drew his sword and ran the monk through. He immediately regretted his deed but it was too late, the monk was dead, so Sir Roger jumped on Grey Dolphin and galloped off. A hue and cry was raised and Sir Roger lived the next few months as an outlaw.

One morning he happened to be riding his horse along the shores of the Thames Estuary when he saw a magnificent ship lying moored just off the beach. He recognised it as the king's ship and the flags flying showed that the king was on board. Sir Roger turned his horse into the sea and swam it towards the ship. When they reached it, Grey Dolphin was tied safely to the stern and Sir Roger was taken aboard where he went to the king and confessed what he had done. He begged the king to forgive him. Taken by Sir Roger's apparent grief and the daring of the deed he had undertaken in swimming out to the ship, the king pardoned Sir Roger who then remounted his horse and returned to the shore.

By now Grey Dolphin was cold and exhausted and he stumbled on the shore. Sir Roger dismounted. Just then a strange old woman came by and said, 'Sir, that horse which has just saved your life will one day be the cause of your death!' Without a second thought, Sir Roger cut off the horse's head and made his way home where he took up his old life.

About a year later, Sir Roger was again walking along that same bit of seashore having once again lost his temper. He saw a piece of white bone sticking up from the shingle and kicked it as hard as he could. It was bigger and heavier than he had realised and a sharp piece of the bone went through his boot and pierced his toe. When the pain had subsided he dug it out from the shingle and found it was a horse's skull.

Over the next few days Sir Roger's toe, then his foot, and soon his whole leg, swelled up with poison and he died a slow, lingering death during which he realised that the old woman's prophecy had come true, that it was Grey Dolphin's skull he had kicked so Grey Dolphin had, indeed, killed him.

After his death, Sir Roger de Shurland was buried in the abbey church in Minster. His grave can still be seen and at the foot of his effigy is a horse's skull.

THE HORSE MECHANIC

One aspect of being a professional storyteller that people often don't appreciate is that you can spend more time driving to and from the gig than you do actually telling stories. There's a plus side to that, though, because strange things can happen when you spend a lot of time on the road and you can sometimes use those adventures to make more stories.

For instance, you meet all kinds of people who, with the kindest of intentions, can sabotage all your best-laid plans; then there's the complete randomness of traffic and road conditions – weather, congestion, whatever it is. You allow for trouble and there isn't any, and when you don't there is – or there isn't, and you spend the whole time waiting for the jam or worrying about *not* being held up. And, of course, there are the gremlins, which inhabit every piece of machinery that's ever been invented and which wait until the most inopportune moment to make themselves known. So, being 'on the road' can sometimes be like being a participant in a fantastic fairy tale or game show!

Nowadays things are made a bit easier by all the gadgets we have. Cars are more reliable (usually). If we need help we have mobile phones (as long as there's a signal). And we can't get lost because we have a satnav (but I'm sure I could write a whole book called 'Adventures with a Satnav'). This story is something which happened to me years ago before all those useful aids were invented.

I'd been doing a daytime storytelling session and was on my way home. It was getting towards evening, quite dark and very quiet. I was nonchalantly driving along, not taking much notice of anything – you know how you do when the car just drives itself and the miles pass without you being aware of anything, when the car stopped. Not suddenly or dramatically – it just … sort of … drifted … to a halt.

As I say, I hadn't been taking much notice of where I was. It was in the countryside and I hadn't passed through a town or village for a while. It was on back roads, so if I needed to summon help I couldn't even give them a road number!

I know nothing about cars at all. I can drive them, but why they do what they do is a mystery. I knew I hadn't run out of petrol but I suppose other things can go wrong too. So I got out of the car and stood there like a spare part wondering what to do and, basically, waiting for something to happen, for my guardian angel to come along – or the AA, or a breakdown truck, or just someone who knew about cars, anything like that would have done.

Nowadays I would have had my mobile phone, but not then, it was before many people had them – just 'yuppies' (remember them?). I suppose I was trying to remember whether I'd seen a phone box or a garage or something recently. No help miraculously appeared, so I had ample time to look around – the trouble was there was nothing to see, just fields and hedges, trees, countryside …

Then, after a while, I heard a voice, from out of nowhere. It said, 'Open the bonnet.'

That seemed a good idea: if your car breaks down open the bonnet … so I did and I stood there because I had no idea what to do next – I just stood there looking into the engine. Then the voice said, 'Take the hose off the carburetter.'

'What's the carburetter look like?' I wondered, but anyway I found a thing with hoses on and took one off and held it in my hand.

I had a really good look around to see who was giving me this advice, but there was no one to be seen.

'Blow down it then,' said the voice.

So I put one end of it in my mouth and blew and – pphht! – a bit of grit flew out of the other end. The wheels in my brain whirred and made connections. 'Ah,' I thought, 'a blocked fuel pipe, I've heard of that.' So I put the hose back on and tried to start the car. Sure enough – brrrm, brrrm – it started first time. Well, I didn't dare turn the engine off again just in case that was tempting providence, but I wanted to know who was this invisible car mechanic that was giving me the advice, so I got out of the car and had a really good look around. Under the hedge, in the ditch, behind the car, in the field – everywhere. But there was no one to be seen.

I couldn't stand around all night so I got in and drove off down the road.

As I drove along I was thinking about what had happened, and the more I thought about it the weirder it got. Who was it giving me the advice? Why couldn't I see him? Was it the Phantom AA man? No, I don't believe in fairies or ghosts but this was really weird …

Then I saw a pub up ahead and I thought, 'I need a drink', so I stopped and went into the bar. There were two old blokes in the bar. They looked as though they were always in the bar, part of the furniture, and after I'd downed my pint we got talking and I told them what had happened. They looked at each other and one of them tapped his nose knowingly. 'Where you broke down,' he said, 'was there a horse in the field?'

I thought about it. 'Yes, I think so,' I said.

'What colour was it?'

'White, I think.'

'Oh, then it's your lucky day,' he said. 'There's usually a black horse in that field and he doesn't know anything about cars at all!'

9

HARES, HORSES AND HEDGEHOGS

The hare is one of the most magical, most mysterious and, in many ways, one of the most loved animals in the countryside. There is a huge amount of modern pagan lore about hares, much of which claims to go back to the distant past. There are hare stories in many other cultures, but not many in Britain – and those all tend to be variations on the same theme: the witch or fairy who can take on hare form. It's a very old story. Here's an Irish version:

OISIN AND THE HARE

Oisin is a hero from Irish mythology. He was the son of the semi-divine hero, Finn mac Cumhaill (Finn McCool).

The story says that one day Oisin was out hunting on the moors when he flushed out a hare. He shot an arrow at it but only managed to wound it on the leg. The hare ran off into some bushes and Oisin followed. Hidden away in the dense undergrowth he found a doorway which opened into a cave and an underground passageway diving down into the earth. He followed the passage until he came out into a huge cavern, where he found a beautiful woman bleeding from a wound in her leg ...

THE HEATHFIELD HARE

A Tale from the West Country

Heathfield is a solitary place, a lonely hamlet surrounded by empty, barren moorland. It was, and still is, the kind of place where the imagination can run riot and people can see all sorts of things – including witches and pixies and magical hares.

One day an old woman made a mistake. She thought it was morning, so she got out of bed, got dressed and prepared to go into town, to market. She put on her cloak, put the panniers on her pony and set off. It was a mistake because it wasn't morning, it was midnight! Perhaps it was the full moon which made her think it was daylight.

As she crossed the moor she heard the sound of hunting horns blowing in the distance and the belling of hounds. Suddenly a hare appeared and veered towards her. When it got close it leapt on to the hedge where she was able to reach out, grab it by the ears, and bundle it into a pannier.

The woman had not gone much further when she saw a sight that chilled her to the core. Coming across the moor towards her was a headless black horse and on its back sat a rider with little horns poking out from under his cap. When she looked further she saw that in one stirrup was a booted foot, but in the other was a cloven hoof. A forked tail hung down over the horse's rump. This rider was surrounded by hounds that gave off a faint luminous light, and around the whole group was a sulphurous smell. The woman knew exactly who she was dealing with.

But, however powerful the Devil might be, he is not infallible, and he doffed his cap and politely asked the old woman if she had seen which way the hare had gone. The woman normally made a point of being truthful and honest but she thought there was no sin in telling lies to the Father of all Lies so she said no, she hadn't seen it.

When she had gone a little further she became aware of movement in the pannier and, to her surprise, the lid opened and there emerged a beautiful young woman dressed all in green. She told the old woman not to be afraid and thanked her for saving her from an unimaginable fate.

'I am not of this earth,' she said, 'but because of a great wrong done many years ago I was doomed to spend my days being hunted, either on the earth or below it, until I could outwit the hunters and get behind their tails while they went searching for me in the wrong direction. Now, thanks to you, I have achieved that and can rest in peace. In return I would like to reward you. From now on all your hens will lay two eggs, where once they laid one, and your cows will give an endless supply of milk. As well as that you will be able to talk twice as much as you did before and your husband will never be able to win an argument. But I must also give you a warning: beware of the Devil. He is a great cheater, but when he finds out that you were clever enough to cheat him he won't like it and will be looking for a way to get his own back. Beware of him and remember that he can take on any form, other than that of a lamb or a dove.'

With that, the green lady vanished and the old woman went on her way to market where she did good trading and went on to live out her days very comfortably.

People around Heathfield still remember her and her story and also know that because Christ was the lamb, and the Holy Spirit the dove, the Evil One can never take on those shapes.

HARE OR HUMAN

There was once an old woman who came up with a good way of making money. Whenever she was running short of cash she would send out her grandson to the local huntsman to tell him that he had seen a hare at a particular location. Without fail the huntsman would reward the boy with a sixpence (which was quite a lot of money for poor people in those days) and then call out the hounds, which always saw the hare disappearing into the distance but were never able to catch it.

When this had happened too many times for it to be coincidence, the huntsman and the other gentlemen involved began to suspect that someone was taking them for fools. It was almost as if the hare knew the hounds would be coming … and where did the hare manage to disappear to?

'The Devil is in the dance,' they thought, 'there is some trickery involved here.' So the local powers that be, including a Justice of the Peace and the vicar, laid their plans. If the Devil was involved then surely the combined powers of Church and State should be able to overcome him. Gradually they began to see how it was done and they decided to lay a trap.

They realised that the boy always reported the hare at about the same time of day, so the huntsman made sure that his hounds were ready and could be loosed instantly. A neighbour kept watch on the old woman's cottage and as soon as she and her grandson left together he was ready to run and alert the huntsman.

After a few days of waiting the trap was sprung. The old woman and her son left her house and then split up, the boy heading towards the huntsman and the old woman towards the spot where the hare would be seen. Almost before the boy had delivered his message the hounds were off and came up upon the hare far sooner than expected. The chase was fast and close, so much so that the poor boy gave himself away by crying out, 'Run, Granny, Run!'

The hounds followed the hare right up to the old woman's house, where it squeezed through a hole at the bottom of the door which was too small to allow them to follow. The hunters attempted to break the door down but her magic would not allow them to, until the vicar and the justice arrived. They went in and upstairs to the bedroom where they found the old woman still out of breath and covered in scratches and cuts from the chase. She denied she was a witch or that she had been the hare, but when they threatened to bring the hounds up to her room to let them decide whether she was hare or human she admitted it. The local inhabitants wanted to duck her but her grandson fell on his knees, sobbing and pleading for his grandmother's life and in the end she was let off with a good whipping.

That wasn't quite the end of the story, though, for a few years later she was again caught and accused of witchcraft and this time she was taken before a very stern judge who sentenced her to be burned at the stake.

THE KENNET VALLEY WITCH

So she became a little mare
As dark as the night was black;
But he became a golden saddle
And he clung on to her back.

(Song: 'The Two Magicians')

There are many stories about animal transformations – animals which become human, or humans who become animal. In some the animal form is 'good', in some it is definitely not!

As we have just seen, one of the most common folk tales found all over Britain is of a witch who transforms herself into an animal, or who transforms the object of her spite into an animal. Often a clever person then manages to injure or mark her in some way while she is in her disguise so that her identity is proved when she returns to her human form. Here is a version from the Kennet Valley in Wiltshire/Berkshire. It is an area jam-packed with ancient archae-ology and history, so it is not surprising that old beliefs and tales linger on there. This story was told around 1902.

There were two farm workers who shared a cottage. One was a carter and the other a thatcher. Their cottage was just a tiny, thatched building for which the term 'cottage' was almost too grand! It had just one room up and one room down plus a tiny lean-to kitchen added on the back. Because it was so small the two men shared everything, including meals and the bed. Although they lived together and worked for the same master the two men were entirely different. The thatcher was a tall, strong man with a ruddy complexion. He looked the picture of health. The carter, though, was bent and weedy and never had any energy. He almost didn't have the strength to get out of bed in the morning and would often fall asleep on the cart. When that happened, the horses were usually able to find their way on their own so it didn't really matter.

One morning the thatcher said, 'Isn't it strange that we eat the same food and sleep in the same bed and do similar work for the same master and yet we're so different.'

'You'd be as bad as me if you were ridden all night as hard as I am,' replied the carter, and went on to explain that every night a witch came and put a bridle on him and rode him about like a horse.

Now the thatcher was sorry for his friend and offered to help. He was a big, powerful man so he suggested that the next night they should change sides in the bed. Then, when the witch came she would have to contend with him!

That night they did as he said and, sure enough, the witch came and saddled and bridled the thatcher and rode him all around the neighbourhood. At last she took him into a stable and tied him up with a lot of other horses who, he realised, must also be poor men who had been bewitched in their sleep by other witches.

When they were left alone the thatcher pulled off the enchanted bridle and hid under the manger. When the witch returned he leapt out and put the bridle on her instead. Then he rode her hard towards home. But on the way he stopped at a blacksmith's. He woke the sleeping blacksmith, who complained loudly and long but eventually gave in and agreed to put a new shoe on the horse's left forefoot. When this had been done the thatcher rode her home and left her outside the farmhouse.

The next day the two men went to their work as usual and the thatcher met the farmer strolling around looking very worried. 'It's my wife,' he said, 'she's ill and won't get up.'

'Make her get up,' said the thatcher, but the farmer couldn't.

'Then make her put her left hand out of bed,' said the thatcher, but again the farmer said she refused. 'Make her,' said the thatcher, 'and if she won't then pull it out from the covers yourself.'

When the farmer eventually made her uncover her hand there was a great iron horseshoe on it and he knew immediately what it meant. 'I thought I was married to a good woman,' he lamented, 'but in fact I'm married to a devil!'

I don't know exactly what he did, but the farmer was soon free of his wife, who was never seen again, and everybody, including the carter, lived much more happily.

THE HEDGEHOG AND THE DEVIL

'Off we go again,' the hedgehog said to the Devil.

You all, no doubt, know of the race between the hare and the tortoise, the story Aesop told to warn against being too cock-sure of your own ability. Here is a variation:

One day Hedgehog made a bet with the Devil that he could beat him in a race. It was agreed that they would meet at night in a ploughed field and run up and down the furrows until one of them had had enough and gave up. Hedgehog, however, got his brother to help him. He stationed his brother at the other end of the course and then he and the Devil lined up and someone shouted, 'Go!'.

Hedgehog didn't move, but the Devil ran as fast as he could to the other end of the field where Hedgehog's brother poked up his head and said, 'Off we go again.' The Devil skidded to a halt and ran back the way he'd come as fast as he could to where the first hedgehog was waiting. 'Off we go again,' he said. And in this way they ran the Devil to death.

10

MAGICAL
TRANSFORMATIONS

So she became a duck
A-floating on the pond
And he became a shaggy old drake
And he chased her round and round.
And she became a sheep
A-laying on the common
And he became a shaggy old ram
And he quickly fell upon her.

(From the 'Two Magicians')

THE SMALL-TOOTH DOG

A Derbyshire version of 'Beauty and the Beast' collected by Sydney Oldall Addy in the last years of the nineteenth century.

Once upon a time there was a merchant who travelled all over the country buying and selling. He also owned a fleet of ships and sometimes travelled far away over the seas to strange countries in search of more exotic goods to trade. When he was on one of these journeys he was attacked by bandits who carried off all his goods and money. His life was only saved thanks to a small-tooth dog which happened to come on the scene at just the right moment and frightened the bandits off.

The dog took the merchant to his house, which was very grand, and he dressed the merchant's wounds and looked after him until he was fully recovered from his ordeal. When the time came for him to leave the merchant said he would like to give the dog something as a token of his thanks and to show how grateful he was. 'Will you accept from me a fish I have which can speak twelve languages?' asked the merchant.

'No, I will not,' said the dog.

'Then will you accept from me a goose which lays golden eggs?' asked the merchant.

'No, I will not,' growled the dog.

'Then will you accept from me a mirror in which you can see what people are really thinking?'

'No,' said the dog, 'I will not.'

'Then what can I offer you?' asked the merchant.

'I will have the thing you hold most dear,' said the dog. 'Bring me your only daughter!'

When he heard this the merchant was very sorry, for his daughter was truly the thing he held most dear. 'In that case,' said the merchant, 'give me one week after I have returned home in which to spend time with my daughter and to take my leave of her, and then you may come and fetch her.'

The dog agreed, and sure enough at the end of the week he came and knocked on the door of the merchant's house. His daughter had been told about the bargain and, although she wasn't very pleased with the idea, she was prepared to go with the dog for her father's sake. She came out of the house and climbed on to the dog's back and he ran off like the wind, back to his own house. The merchant's daughter stayed with the dog for a month and was treated very well and was quite comfortable in his grand house, but towards the end of that time she started to feel homesick and she moped around the house looking very unhappy.

When the dog asked her what the matter was, she said that she wanted to go to see her father. The dog agreed, saying that she could go, on condition that she only stay for three days. 'But before I let you go,' said the dog, 'what do you call me?'

'A great, foul, small-tooth dog,' she replied.

'Then,' said the dog, 'I will not let you go.' The girl cried so much at this that the dog relented and said he would take her after all. 'But what do you call me?' he asked.

'Your name is As-sweet-as-a-honeycomb,' said the girl, happily.

'Then jump up on my back and I'll carry you home.'

When they were well on the way back to the merchant's house they came to a stile. The dog slowed. 'What do you call me?' he asked.

'A great, foul, small-tooth dog,' said the girl, thinking that they were nearly home.

'Then,' said the dog, 'I will not let you go.' And he didn't jump over the stile but turned and ran back towards his house. They stayed at the dog's house for another full week and the girl again begged the dog to take her home. 'What do you call me?' he asked.

'Your name is As-sweet-as-a-honeycomb,' said the girl.

'Then jump up on my back and I'll carry you home.'

So the girl got on the dog's back and off they ran. When they got to the stile the dog asked, 'What do you call me?'

'Your name is As-sweet-as-a-honeycomb,' said the girl, and on they ran until they came to a second stile.

By now they were almost within sight of the merchant's house, so when the dog asked, 'What do you call me?' she did not think he would turn round and take her all the way back again.

'A great, foul, small-tooth dog,' she said.

The dog growled and leapt in the air and turned and ran at top speed back to his house where they stayed for another full week. After she had cried and moped around all that week she again begged the dog to take her home, and he agreed. So she mounted upon his back again and off they ran. When they got to the first stile he asked, 'What do you call me?'

'As-sweet-as-a-honeycomb,' and the dog jumped over the first stile.

When they got to the second stile he asked, 'What do you call me?'

'As-sweet-as-a-honeycomb,' and the dog jumped over the second stile.

When they got to the gate of the merchant's house he again asked, 'What do you call me?'

And the girl started to say 'A great f ...', but she saw the sad look which started to come over the dog's face and she felt him hesitate and start to turn so she said, 'As-sweet-as-a-honeycomb.' And the dog walked up to the door of the house and the girl dismounted from his back and rang the doorbell. She expected the dog to leave her and run off back to his own house and come back in three days' time, but to her surprise, he stood up on his hind legs and reached up and pulled off his dog's head and then he wriggled and shook and stepped out of his dog's coat and there stood the finest young nobleman the girl had ever seen.

And, as you can no doubt guess, they were soon married and, to prove this is a fairy tale, they all lived happily ever after.

The idea of someone being disguised by a 'second skin' which they can put on or take off is very common in folklore all over the world. In this collection it includes silkies, frog princes and were-wolves! Where did the idea come from? I once read a description

*of travellers in Russia who looked like huge bears with all their
fur coats and mittens and hats, but when they dismounted from
their troikas and entered a house they shed them and emerged in
all their glory, like a butterfly emerging from a chrysalis. Perhaps
that's a clue.*

THE SEAL WIFE

One evening a fisherman was walking home along the beach.
It was a beautiful ending to the day, with the sun casting its
long rays over the sea and making dark shadows on the white
sand. Here and there large outcrops of rock stood up from the
flat sand and in some places there were rock pools and crops of
seaweed. It was a quiet, lonely place and the fisherman did not
expect to meet anyone else on the beach. He lived alone in the
little house in which his father and grandfather had also lived
and where he had been born.

He was surprised then, when he became aware of voices. It
sounded like a laugh and a giggle and a scream of merriment and
it was coming from the next cove, just behind another outcrop
of rocks. Not knowing what to expect, he crouched behind the
rocks and carefully peeped out into the cove. There he saw two
beautiful young women playing in the evening light. They were
skipping and leaping and chasing each other and all the while
laughing. They were both stark naked. He was bewitched by
their beauty and for a moment could do nothing but look.

Then the fisherman guessed who or what the young women
were, and this was borne out when he saw two seal skins lying
carefully folded on the sand quite near to his hiding place.
They were silkies – seal women. In the sea they looked and
behaved like ordinary seals, but they were able to come out of

the sea and take off their seal skins to reveal a human form. He knew from all the old stories he'd heard ever since he was a boy that if he could take her seal skin the silkie would be trapped in her human form and he could have her for his wife.

The fisherman crept out from his hiding place and sneaked towards the skins, but the women saw him, screamed and raced to retrieve them. One of them did so, but the other, who had been slightly further away, was unable to get to the skin before the fisherman had it in his hand. The first woman scrambled into her skin and flopped into the water where she watched from a safe distance with tears falling from her huge seal eyes. The other woman fell on her knees and cried. She grasped the fisherman round the ankles and begged for her skin to be returned. But the fisherman wanted a wife so he ignored her pleas, took her arm, and dragged her off to his house. There, he gave her some clothes to wear and went to hide the seal skin away in a shed.

The couple lived together for many years and she bore him two sons. They were reasonably happy in their different ways – at least as happy as many couples who are far more similar to each other. The only thing that showed that the seal wife might not be entirely reconciled to her life was the fact that she would sometimes steal away to walk by the sea. Sometimes she sat on the rocks and sang in a strange tongue, but only when

there was no chance of anyone hearing her, and her song was sometimes answered by a particularly large bull seal who was often seen swimming off the beach where the fisherman had found his seal wife.

One day, when her eldest son was about ten years old, the boys were playing in the old sheds and outhouses because it was raining and blowing a gale. In their play they moved some old chests and boxes and one of them fell down and split open to reveal a seal skin. The boys wondered what it was doing hidden away in a box, but they also thought it was beautiful and took it to show their mother. They knew she would like it, but she was overcome with emotion and alternated between joy and sorrow. She skipped around the room laughing with joy but all the while tears ran down her cheeks. Then she hugged her children and wished them goodbye and raced off to the shore with the folded seal skin under her arm.

When the fisherman came home he found the house empty and no supper waiting for him. He found his sons and asked where his wife was. When the boys told him what had happened he raced down to the beach just in time to see a female seal sliding into the water where a large bull seal was waiting to greet her. The two creatures swam and leapt and embraced in a welter of joy, and when they had exhausted themselves they swam slowly into the shallows. The seal wife then addressed her earthbound husband and said, 'Farewell, and may all good attend you. I loved you well enough when I was your wife but I always loved my first husband so much better. Now I have returned to him. Look after our children and wish them well from me. I promise that neither you nor they will ever come to harm on the sea.'

Then the two seals turned and dived beneath the waves and were never seen again.

The fisherman lived to a ripe old age and his sons took over his boat and made a good living at fishing. When the time came, their sons took their turn and throughout all those years all the men in that family seemed to have an uncanny gift for knowing where the fish would be. They never returned to shore with empty holds and none of them ever perished in the stormy seas. They had a reputation for being 'lucky'.

Tales of silkies are well known all around the coasts of Scotland and Ireland.

11

Exotic Animals

The Woman Who Married a Bear

As I mentioned in the introduction, the canon of stories is always in need of topping up and renewal. This is not truly a 'British' folk tale, although I'd love it to become one. It's a story I've been telling for at least two decades and it is always a 'hit'. When I first came across it, I wasn't sure where it came from; I guessed it wasn't British but thought it might be European, possibly Scandinavian. I was correct about the latitude, but way out on the longitude, for it is actually Native American. It sits very well in a British context though, and I tell it as if it is happening in the North of England or southern Scotland – apart from the bears!

Once upon a time, on a bright summer's morning, a young noblewoman went out picking blackberries. She'd found and collected a lot of them and had a big basketful ready to take home, when she found another blackberry bush which had the biggest, juiciest berries she'd yet found, so she just had to top her basket up with those. When she was almost finished she saw a bramble at the very top of the bush with even larger, juicier berries on and she had to have some of those as well. They were possibly the best-looking blackberries she'd ever seen, but they were almost out of reach. She stood on tiptoe and she reached up ... and she stretched ... and she could just about touch the berries, but couldn't quite get hold of them ... so she stretched just a little more ... and her feet slipped from under her and she fell down on to her back and spilled blackberries everywhere.

She sat up and looked around and swore to herself. Then she saw why she'd slipped. She had put her foot in some bear dung and now it was on her shoe and up her leg and on the hem of her dress. To make matters worse, the bears responsible had obviously been gorging on blackberries too for the bear dung was full of sticky, purple juice. She cursed the bears and their forebears for as far back in history as she could imagine, and then scrambled to her feet and began to retrieve her spilled blackberries.

Unfortunately for the young woman the two bears responsible for her mishap happened to be on the other side of the bush, sleeping off their blackberry feast. The crash of her falling down woke them up and they heard her cursing them and they were angry. They got up, went round the bush, grabbed the young woman by the arms and took her back to the village where the bears lived. There they took her before the chief bear and reported what she'd said. The bears were angry and wanted her punished.

The chief bear ordered that she should be taken and shut up in a cave until he made up his mind what to do with her. She was put in the cave and a big rock was rolled across the entrance. She found herself in utter darkness. It did not bode well! 'Oh, this is a real mess you've got yourself into,' she said to herself. 'I don't know how you are going to get out of this.'

Then from the darkness a voice answered her, 'If you want to escape with your life you'd better do everything I tell you.' In the gloom she saw that it was a tiny mouse. The mouse told her to take off the necklace she was wearing and smash it up with a stone until it was just little bits, like gravel.

'I couldn't do that,' she said in a shocked voice, 'it's a family heirloom; it's gold, it's been in my family for generations.'

'If you want to escape with your life you'd better do exactly what I tell you,' repeated the mouse.

With tears trickling down her cheeks the young woman took off the necklace, laid it on a flat rock and then, with a large stone, pounded it to pieces. Then the mouse told her the rest of the plan.

She waited for an hour or two and then began to put it into operation. First she called out to the bears, 'Hello, bears! Is anybody there? Can you hear me?' When she was eventually answered she explained that she needed to answer a 'call of nature'. (She said it very politely and primly as befitted a noblewoman!) She said that she didn't know how long she was going to be shut up there in the cave so she didn't want to do anything smelly and unpleasant there. She asked whether the bears would take her down into the forest so that she could go there, behind a tree. She promised that she wouldn't try to run away.

She heard the bears grunt and go away, but soon they came back and the stone was rolled away from the entrance. Three bears took her down into the forest and waited while she went behind a tree. There she scraped a small hole in the ground and crouched down and did what she needed to do. Then she reached into her apron pocket and took out some of the broken pieces of gold necklace and sprinkled them over what she'd done. Then she covered it all over with pine needles and leaves and went back to the bears looking satisfied. Two of them took her back to the cave while the third had a good sniff around. He scraped open the hole she'd so carefully covered and …

He didn't believe it! What's this? This woman shits gold!

As fast as he could he ran back to the chief bear and told him what he'd found. The chief bear was puzzled, and interested, and fascinated. He didn't know what it meant, so he ordered that the woman was not to be harmed, but that she was to be fed and kept in the cave until further notice.

The next day the woman repeated the trick and, sure enough, the bears really did seem to have discovered a woman who shits gold! Now you don't harm someone like that, so they looked after her. They treated her well. They gave her increasing amounts of freedom. Every now and again she repeated the ritual, just to make sure they didn't change their minds.

As the summer passed she was allowed to wander around the village of the bears as she wished. As long as she did not go too far away she was able to go where she pleased. She found that she was accepted by the bears and she began to think of some of them as friends. She gossiped with the female bears and played with their cubs. Most of the male bears had little to do with her, but there was one good-looking young bear with whom she got on very well. When the days grew shorter and there began to be frosts at night he brought her a gift, a pure white bearskin to wrap herself in. By midwinter they had moved in together and he had become her husband.

The couple lived happily in the village of the bears all through the long winter and when spring came she gave birth to two beautiful baby bear cubs. She loved her family and they were all happy and carefree until, one morning, two bears who had been out foraging came back and said they'd heard the sounds of hounds and hunters. She knew instantly who it was. It was her human family, her father and her brothers, seeking her. And she knew what would happen if they found her with the bears – they would all be slaughtered and the village burned to the ground.

The young woman and her little family took their leave of the bears and set out to escape from the hunters. Every day they travelled as far and as fast as they could, and when night fell they slept in a cave or a hollow tree or under some bushes. But although they travelled as fast as they could, every morning when they awoke, the belling of the hounds was nearer, and the shouting of the hunters was louder.

At last, one morning, they awoke to find the hounds snuffling around the edges of the clearing in which they had slept. She knew the chase was over. Escape was impossible. But she also knew that she would be alright. They would not harm her, and she thought that she could probably plead for the lives of her two baby bears, but she could think of no way of saving her husband bear. The anger of her human family would be too great.

In the end they agreed on a compromise. A truce was announced in which husband bear would teach his wife and the two baby bears and all the members of her family how to do the Bear Dance. When they had all learned it to his satisfaction then he would allow them to kill him.

This was done and the young noblewoman took her two baby bears and returned to her human family's home. She went through the usual processes of grieving that everyone goes through after a death, or at the end of a love affair, but time passed and healed, and after a while she fell in love with a young man and later gave birth to two baby boys who were just as perfect as the two baby bear cubs had been. In turn the baby bears grew up and decided they wanted to return to their own kind in the forest, which they did.

The boys grew up happily and, when they were old enough, they were taught the Bear Dance. Since then it has been passed down through that family to every succeeding generation

and at last it was my turn to learn it. Although you are not a member of the family I could teach you how to do it – it's a great dance and great fun to do, but we can't do it on the pages of a book so you'll have to wait until we meet at a live gig! Meanwhile the picture will give you some idea of it.

ALLIGATORS

Most of the stories in this collection are 'traditional', which usually means 'old'. But all traditional stories must have been new at some time. I am proud to say that I was responsible for, if not the creation of this story, at least its transmission. Many years ago I came across a tiny (four lines?) joke in a magazine. I liked it and grew it into a story. It proved popular, and with input from audiences – and witty hecklers, etc. – it grew even more.

I've told it many times and included it in the Facts & Fiction *storytelling magazine. It was also included in a collection put together about twenty years ago by Birmingham Libraries. Other people have obviously picked it up and told it because, quite recently, it came back to me in an Australian version! It was not a very good telling and was rather racist, but the 'hero' – the boy who swims – was 'Colin, the Aborigine', and instead of a lake it was an urban swimming pool!*

There was once a king who had a daughter who was just coming to marriageable age. In those days and in that place girls had to be married, even princesses – or especially princesses. They did not usually have much of a say as to who their marriage partner would be, their parents just arranged it and then announced it, and that was the end of it.

Now this king loved his daughter very much and wanted the best for her. He wanted to find her a husband who would make her happy, someone about her own age who would be kind to her and treat her well. It didn't matter whether the young man was rich or not because, eventually, he and the princess would inherit all the king's wealth, along with the kingdom. It was more important that he was healthy and strong and, if possible, good-looking. In other words, that he was someone the princess could live happily with.

How was he to find this young man? The king and his advisors put their heads together and came up with a plan. They would hold a competition – an athletic competition. If he was good at sport he was probably healthy and that often goes with good looks … but what kind of sport?

In their kingdom was a popular beauty spot called the Long Lake, which was just that, a long lake, so what better than a swimming competition? Now anyone (almost) could swim across the lake, but swimming all the way down the whole length of it would make a suitable task. So they decided that there would be a swimming competition at the Long Lake and the winner would get the princess's hand in marriage.

But then someone raised the point that there might be a really good swimmer who didn't want to marry the princess. He wouldn't enter the competition and they really did need all the best swimmers in the race. They didn't want to devalue it. So they decided there should be a choice of prizes: they were certain that the winner would want to marry the princess, but just so that no one was put off, if they didn't want to marry the princess then they could have half the kingdom; and if, by any chance they didn't want half the kingdom, then they could have as much gold as they could carry away in two carrier bags. That would solve the problem, they were sure.

So the king sent out his messengers and heralds all around the kingdom and into all the neighbouring kingdoms to announce that at midday on 1 August there would be a swimming competition at the Long Lake, the prize for the winner being the princess's hand in marriage (and in the unlikely case that he didn't want that, half the kingdom or as much gold as he could carry away in two carrier bags).

When 1 August came the shores of the Long Lake were thronged with people. There had never been such crowds before. There were all the young men who were going to swim, and all their friends and families coming to cheer them on; there were local people just coming to watch and see what happened; and there were people out to make a bit of money – jugglers and fire-eaters, poets and storytellers, women reading fortunes, bookmakers taking bets, and men selling hot dogs and hamburgers. It was a whole big festival which you could hear and smell a mile off.

At noon a hush fell over the crowd and the royal party made their way on to the dais. Trumpets blared and the prime minister gave a little speech and announced what was going to happen. The signal for the race to start, he said, was when the king said, 'On your marks, get set, GO!' and dropped his handkerchief. All the while he was speaking young men were getting ready – taking off their shoes, unbuttoning their jackets, stretching their limbs and taking deep breaths.

Just then the king himself interrupted. 'To make this all a bit more interesting,' he said, 'I have recently stocked the lake with alligators!'

Silence.

Not a sound, as everyone turned to look.

And then they saw what they hadn't seen before: that log floating in the water had little legs paddling away beneath it; the old tree stump laying on the shore had little eyes … the more they looked the more alligators they could see and they were the biggest, meanest-looking alligators any of them had ever seen.

Then the king shouted, 'On your marks, get set, GO!' and dropped his handkerchief …

… And nothing happened.

No one dived into the water.

No young men started swimming.

In fact, various young men were buttoning up their coats which had 'accidentally' come undone, or were tying their shoe-laces which they didn't want to trip over. They'd never had any intention of swimming themselves, they'd just come to watch.

All the old men were in a huddle complaining away as old men are wont to do. 'Young people today,' they grumbled, 'it's not like when we were young. We wouldn't have worried about a few alligators. We'd have swum up there so quickly we'd have been out at the other end before the alligators had even thought about it. If they had caught us we would have wrestled with them like Tarzan … they wouldn't have stood a chance against us. I blame these here computers, they rot your brain … all that fiddling with your joystick it's not natural … blah, blah, blah.'

And while everyone was looking the other way there was a sudden splash! There in the water was a young man. Off up the lake he went with his legs kicking and his arms going like windmills. A huge cheer went up.

He was a quarter of the way up the lake and the alligators had seen him.

Halfway up the lake and they were sliding into the water.

Three-quarters of the way up the lake and they were getting closer and closer.

Nine-tenths of the way up the lake and the leading alligator's mouth was open ready to bite.

And the young man leapt out on to the shore at the far end, just as the alligator's jaws clamped shut and missed him by a hair's breadth. A huge cheer went up and everyone gathered round and patted him on the back. They put a blanket round his shoulders and led him back to the king, who shook his hand and kissed him on both cheeks. 'Congratulations,' he said. 'You were the only one who was brave enough to swim against the alligators. Would you like to marry my daughter?'

'No, I don't want that,' said the young man, and a great sigh went round the crowd.

'Then you must want half the kingdom.'

'No, I don't want that either.' So was he just a greedy young man who wanted as much gold as he could carry away in two carrier bags? 'No, I don't want that,' he said.

That puzzled everyone, including the king. 'But you jumped into the lake and you risked your life swimming up there with the alligators after you, you must want something,' said the king.

The young man turned and faced the crowd. He looked round it staring deep into everyone's eyes. 'Yes,' he said. 'I want to know which of you is the rotten so-and-so who pushed me in!'

THE WONDERFUL CROCODILE!

Now list ye, landsmen, all to me,
To tell the truth I'm bound,
What happened to me by going to sea
And the wonders that I found.
Shipwrecked was I once off Perouse
And cast all on the shore,
So I resolved to take a cruise,
The country to explore.

[Chorus] Tol-lol, tol-lol, little-tol-lol
The Wonderful Crocodile

But far I had not scuddied out,
When close alongside the ocean,
I saw something move, which at first I thought
Was all the world in motion.
By steering close up alongside
I saw it was a crocodile;

And from the end of his nose to the tip of his tail
It measured five hundred mile.

This crocodile I could plainly see
Was none of the common race,
For I had to climb up a very high tree
Before I could see his face.
And when he lifted up his jaw,
(Tho' perhaps you'll think it a lie)
His back was three miles through the clouds
And his nose near touched the sky.

Oh, up aloft the wind was high,
It blew a gale from the south;
I lost my hold and away I flew
Right into the crocodile's mouth.
He quickly closed his jaws on me,
He thought to grab a victim;
But I slipped down his throat, d'ye see,
And that's the way I tricked 'im.

I travelled on for a month or two
Till I got into his maw,
Where I found rum kegs not a few
And a thousand bullocks in store.
Of life I banished all my cares
For in grub I wasn't stinted;
And in this crocodile I lived seven years,
Very well contented.

This crocodile being very old,
One day, alas, he died;

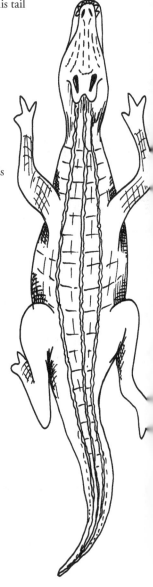

But he was three years getting cold,
He was so long and wide.
His skin was ten miles thick, I'm sure,
Or very near about;
For I was full six months or more
Cutting a hole to get out.

So now once more I'm safe on earth,
Resolved no more to roam.
In a ship that passed I got a berth,
And now I'm safe at home.
But, if my story you should doubt,
Should you ever travel the Nile
Just where he fell you'll find the shell
Of this wonderful crocodile.

This tall tale was widely printed on broadsides on both sides of the Atlantic back in the nineteenth century. The crocodile is remarkably similar to 'Assipattle's Muckle Mester Stoorworm'.

THE TALE OF TOMMY THE TORTOISE

From monstrous reptiles to cute ones!

I was born and brought up a Man of Kent – my father's family have lived there 'for ever'. I left when I was 18, well before I got into folk music and storytelling, but I have accumulated quite a few Kentish folk songs since. Stories are another matter, though. I've never set out to seriously research any, but neither have I come across many good ones in the usual run of being a storyteller. This is one of the few I've found.

Tommy the Tortoise lived with his Mum Tortoise and his Dad Tortoise and his little sister Tilly Tortoise in a lovely little Kentish village where the houses had timbered walls and thatched roofs and where there were hop fields and oast houses. Tommy was a lively, clever young tortoise, always up to mischief, and it was very difficult to put one over on him.

One summer's day the Tortoise family decided to go for a picnic, so Mum Tortoise packed up everything they would need into a big hamper which Dad Tortoise then strapped to his shell. While they were doing this, the two children Tortoises scampered around as fast as tortoises can scamper.

Then they set off and they walked and walked for a long while until they came to what Dad Tortoise said was, 'A nice place for a picnic'. (*We* would have thought that they hadn't gone very far, but not very far for us is a long way for a tortoise!)

Dad unstrapped the hamper from his shell and Mum spread out the rugs and started to unpack the food. There were sandwiches and tomatoes and radishes and lots and lots of lettuce. There were also bottles of lemonade for the children Tortoises. It was when she took out the bottles of beer that she had packed especially for Dad Tortoise that Mum Tortoise exclaimed, 'Oh no, we've forgotten something vital!'

'What is it?' the children asked.

'The bottle opener. Your Dad won't be able to have his beer without a bottle opener!'

The children didn't think this was very terrible. They thought Dad could drink lemonade like the rest of them, but Mum insisted that Dad deserved his beer, especially after carrying the hamper all that way. And Dad agreed! 'Tommy,' they said, 'you're the fastest. You run back and fetch the bottle opener.'

Tommy didn't want to run back and fetch the bottle opener. 'I know what will happen,' he said, 'as soon as I'm out of sight you'll start eating the sandwiches and by the time I get back there'll be nothing left for me!'

His parents assured him that wouldn't be the case. They promised that they wouldn't eat a bite until he was back with the bottle opener so, grumbling, Tommy the Tortoise trotted off.

Time passed …

'He must be there by now,' said Dad.

'I'm hungry,' said Tilly.

'Don't worry, he'll soon be back,' said Mum.

More time passed …

'He's taking his time,' said Dad.

'I'm very hungry,' said Tilly.

'He won't be long now,' said Mum.

Yet more time passed …

'Couldn't we just have a bite?' asked Tilly.

'We could put Tommy's share aside for him,' said Dad, who was also getting hungry.

'Alright,' said Mum, 'I'll share out the sandwiches and we'll just have one each and then wait until Tommy gets back before we eat the lettuce.'

So Mum Tortoise shared out the sandwiches into four piles and all three of them lifted their first sandwich to their mouths. They had not even had time to take a bite when out from the nearest bush popped Tommy the Tortoise's angry face. 'There, I told you that would happen,' he said. 'It's a good job I didn't go all the way back to get that bottle opener or there would have been nothing left for me at all!'

THE LION SAYS HIS PRAYERS

I'll finish with two stories about people who travelled to far-off lands.

A man was going on safari in Africa and before they left they were given the 'Health and Safety' talk. They were told of all the things they should and shouldn't do once they had left the safety of the city and were out in the wilds. One point that was rammed home with great force was, 'Don't go off on your own!' They were told that they'd be perfectly safe as long as they stayed with everyone else and did what the guides told them.

But, just in case, there was a set of instructions on what to do if you did happen to confront particular wild animals. They were told that if you meet a certain creature you should stand perfectly still because its eyesight is not very good so it probably won't see you; if you meet another one then climb a tree and stay there until help comes; if you meet this animal lay down and play dead because it won't touch a dead body; if you meet that animal make yourself as big as possible and shout and scream and wave your arms about; if you meet that one then … run like hell!

And they were told especially carefully what to do if you meet a lion.

What do you do if you meet a lion? You stare it in the eyes and you copy everything it does.

Fully briefed and equipped with everything they'd possibly need, they set off into the bush. The first night they stopped in a pre-prepared camp where a large campfire blazed and they were served a delicious feast complete with plenty of drink and conversation. As the evening wore on the man felt that he needed to relieve himself. He couldn't really see much point in walking all the way back to the latrine tent, especially as he'd have to call a guide and have an escort, so he slipped away from the fire and round the back of a bush. He unzipped his trousers …

… And then he realised he was not alone! There was a large male lion sprawled on the ground.

What do you do when you come face to face with a lion? He struggled to remember. Oh yes, you stare it in the eyes and you copy everything it does. Easy to say, but harder to do!

The lion sat up and looked at the man. The man looked at the lion.

The lion blinked. The man blinked.

The lion scratched his ear. The man scratched his ear.

The lion yawned. The man yawned.

The lion wagged his tail. The man didn't have a tail but he waved his arm behind his back and hoped that would do.

The lion licked his lips. The man licked his lips.

Then the lion folded its paws in front of itself and closed his eyes. The man put his hands together and closed his eyes (but kept having a surreptitious peep so that he could see what the lion was going to do next).

After a while the lion spoke. 'I don't know what you're praying for,' he said, 'but I'm just saying grace.'

THE TWO ELEPHANTS

Another man, while rambling through the African bush, suddenly came upon an elephant sitting on its backside with its legs held out in front of it – as you sometimes see them when they are performing in the circus ring. He thought it strange, but it had its back to him and it obviously hadn't seen him so the man quietly tiptoed by. However, a short time later he came across another elephant sitting in the same position. This one was facing him and had seen him so he spoke to it and said that he'd just seen another elephant sitting like that and asked what they were doing.

'Shhh ...' replied the elephant, 'Don't disturb us. We're playing bookends!'

THE KNIGHT AND THE DRAGON

You may have seen something like this before! Or have you?
You can keep on telling it to yourself for as long as you like …
and then go back and start the book again, perhaps?

Once upon a time a knight met a dragon.
'I'm going to eat you up,' said the dragon.
'Oh, don't do that,' said the knight, 'and I'll tell you a story.'
So he began:

Once upon a time a knight met a dragon.
'I'm going to eat you up,' said the dragon.
'Oh, don't do that,' said the knight, 'and I'll tell you a story.'
So he began:

Once upon a time a knight met a dragon.
'I'm going to eat you up,' said the dragon.
'Oh, don't do that,' said the knight, 'and I'll tell you a story.'
So he began:

Once upon a time a knight met a dragon.
'I'm going to eat you up,' said the dragon.
'Oh, don't do that,' said the knight, 'and I'll tell you a story.'
So he began:

Once upon a time a knight met a dragon …

INDEX OF PLACES

BIBLIOGRAPHY

The stories in this collection have come from a myriad of different sources: books, magazines, websites, etc. I have often put together bits from different versions but, whatever the actual source, a lot of them can be traced back to one collection:

Joseph Jacobs, *English Fairy Tales* (1890) and *More English Fairy Tales* (1894), available in several editions and online.

Other books which were particularly useful were:

Addy, Sidney Oldall, *Household Tales & Traditional Remains, Collected in the Counties of York, Lincoln, Derby & Nottingham* (David Nutt, 1895). It seems impossible to get hold of a copy of the book but it can be found online at www.archive.org/stream/householdtaleswi00addyrich#page/n9/mode/2up.
Briggs, Katherine M., *A Dictionary of British Folk Tales* (Routledge & Kegan Paul Ltd, 1970).
Crossley-Holland, Kevin (ed.), *Folk Tales of the British Isles* (Faber & Faber, 1985).
Philip, Neil, *The Penguin Book of English Folk Tales* (Penguin Books, 1992).
Westwood, Jennifer & Jacqueline Simpson, *The Lore of the Land* (Penguin Books, 2005).

Many, if not most, of the 'County Folk Tales' series published by The History Press contain other animal folk tales or, more likely, different versions of some of the tales in this book. It's well worth comparing the different tellings.

ABOUT THE AUTHOR

PETE CASTLE was born and brought up in Ashford, Kent. He went to Bretton Hall College of Education in Yorkshire in 1965, where he met his wife Sue. He taught for ten years in Lincolnshire, Nottingham and Luton before going professional as a 'folk singer' in 1978. After a few years he discovered oral storytelling and has continued to do the two in tandem ever since. Although he can limit himself to one or other discipline, he likes to do a mixture of the two whenever possible. Pete has worked all over the UK in folk and storytelling clubs, at festivals, in arts centres, schools and libraries. One of his career highlights was being invited to take part in the Smithsonian Folklife Festival in Washington DC.

In the 1980s Pete ran a highly rated local radio folk show and since 1999 has edited *Facts & Fiction*, which is probably the only independent storytelling magazine in the world. His becoming an author for The History Press probably developed out of this.

Although he now describes himself as 'semi-retired', he continues to keep busy, the difference being that he can pick and choose which gigs he does! Pete and Sue live in Belper in Derbyshire where they are involved in all kinds of community activities.

See Pete's website at www.petecastle.co.uk, and *Facts & Fiction* at www.factsandfiction.co.uk.

BY THE SAME AUTHOR

Books

Derbyshire Folk Tales (The History Press, 2010).

Nottinghamshire Folk Tales (The History Press, 2012).

CDs

Pete has a number of CDs available featuring both songs and stories.
Particularly relevant are *The Derby Ram*, by Pete and other artists, which
features two versions of that famous song, and *Blue Dor* by Popeluc,
which includes 'Reynardine'.

The complete list is on his website at www.petecastle.co.uk.

There are also songs and stories on Pete's YouTube channel at www.youtube.
com/channel/UCq6xTFVShO_jo3Y-Q9rU9Hg/videos.

Magazine

Pete also edits *Facts & Fiction* storytelling magazine –
www.factsandfiction.co.uk.

Society *for*
Storytelling

Since 1993, the Society for Storytelling has championed the art of oral storytelling and the benefits it can provide – such as improving memory more than rote learning, promoting healing by stimulating the release of neuropeptides, or simply great entertainment! Storytellers, enthusiasts and academics support and are supported by this registered charity to ensure the art is nurtured and developed throughout the UK.

Many activities of the Society are available to all, such as locating storytellers on the Society website, taking part in our annual National Storytelling Week at the start of every February, purchasing our quarterly magazine *Storylines*, or attending our Annual Gathering – a chance to revel in engaging performances, inspiring workshops, and the company of like-minded people.

You can also become a member of the Society to support the work we do. In return, you receive free access to *Storylines*, discounted tickets to the Annual Gathering and other storytelling events, the opportunity to join our mentorship scheme for new storytellers, and more. Among our great deals for members is a 30% discount off titles in the *Folk Tales* series from The History Press website.

For more information, including how to join, please visit

www.sfs.org.uk

Lightning Source UK Ltd.
Milton Keynes UK
UKOW06f0103050116

265769UK00002B/3/P